san

from Jean.

July, 1980.

Latakia

Latakia

a novel by
Audrey Thomas

Talonbooks . Vancouver . Los Angeles . 1979

copyright © 1979 Audrey Thomas

published with assistance from the Canada Council

Talonbooks
201 1019 East Cordova
Vancouver
British Columbia V6A 1M8
Canada

Talonbooks
P.O. Box 42720
Los Angeles
California 90042
U.S.A.

This book was typeset by Linda Gilbert, designed by David Robinson and printed by Hemlock Printers for Talonbooks.

First printing: October 1979

Canadian Cataloguing in Publication Data

Thomas, Audrey Callahan, 1935—
    Latakia

    ISBN 0-88922-167-7 pa.

    I. Title.
    PS8539.H64L3   C813'.5'4   C79-091205-8
    PR9199.3.T49L3

To 3663, Jeanne Mance, for the "first firing,"
and to Slug Pottery, Roberts Creek, for the final one,
with love.

And in memory of
Αργγρούλα Ταλαρ῾κι

Epigraph

No matter how we write the word *man*, whether in small letters or large, it never looks like a man; but when we read or pronounce the word, then the word *man* comes out.

Of course this reverence for established orders is not unique with the Egyptians. All human beings tend to keep to the old ways even when they are adding the new.

Oscar Ogg,
The 26 Letters

"When two vowels go walking,
The first one does the talking"

(Old Rhyme Used in Elementary Schools to
Explain the Pronunciation of Words like 'Goat')

Epigraph

English: I can't get over it
Now I've seen everything

France: Je n'en reviens pas
J'aurai tout vu
J'en ai assez

Canada: J'ai mon voyage

from *The Practical Handbook*
of Canadian French

It is Saturday night, "our" night, around seven-thirty. I
have been here for almost one month. The sun is a long way
from down and if I were to climb to the top of the hill above
the village, up past the Hotel Acteon and the Hotel Astoria
(Lux) and the skeletal frames of two new luxury hotels, I
would look down on a sea that flickered blue and yellow, like
gas jets, a sea flambé. I have done this several times since my
return and sat on a rock a little lower down where I have a
clear view of the square, usually pretty deserted at this hour,
for the Beautiful Ones have gone back to their hotels and
"Rent Rooms" to wash away the sea from bodies and hair
and get ready for the evening. There is a giant chess game
outside Zorba's Bar, with squares as big as windows and great
chipped wooden chess pieces, but from the rock where I
might be sitting, the square itself becomes a chessboard
— for it is made up of cement squares — and if I sat long
enough, I could watch that other game. I have never been
to a watering spot before, and when we were here in the
autumn, we went to bed early, even on Saturdays, and so
missed all the fun.

Sometimes I simply gaze out to sea; Africa is only two
hundred miles away. The rock I sit on is rough and warm
against my bare legs. In my memories of Greece, I will always
think of the austerity of the landscape and of rocks: white

15

rocks, black rocks, brown rocks, grey rocks, carved rocks, rocks with weeds growing on them, rocks with monasteries and temples on them, piles of rocks near archaeological digs, rock walls meandering (good Greek word) across the landscape, rocks to stumble over in streets or on mountain paths, rocks rolling into deep ravines, rocks jutting out of the sea and called islands, like this rock, this island, Crete. Rocks everywhere. And the rocky faces of the old people, the rock-coloured donkeys they ride. Beautiful rocks. Everywhere, beautiful rocks.

But tonight, I am content to sit up on my flat roof, drying my hair. I have with me a mirror, a hairbrush, a bottle of ice-cold retsina from the store downstairs and a basket full of your letters. It is an aerogramme. "GREETINGS," it says, and underneath, there is a picture of a snarling leopard. You have been thinking about me, you say, and wondering how I've been doing. KUFUNGUA KATA HAPA. TO OPEN SLIT HERE. You have said it is an easy language, Swahili. WA, wife. MKE, wives. WAKE, good wives. WAKE WAZURI. I had to laugh at your examples. Wives plural, good or otherwise, proved too much for us all.

"It's nine p.m. The African night sounds outside. So strange to imagine you there in Aghia Sophia. I can see it all so well: the grocery store downstairs, the fat woman across the way, the bakery, the post office, the sun coming up over the water, the cafés, George and Yannis, volleyball, the Magic Boat. Are you reading this, perhaps, looking out over the water and sipping ouzo? What a time we had there! And I miss you."

What was Hester doing while you were writing that? Did you stretch and get up and say, "Well, I think I'll just drop a note to Rachel," and go into your study and shut the door? No, you wouldn't shut the door, would you? She might think you were masturbating in there.

I always used to know, on the boat, when you had done that — written to her and masturbated. Your eyes looked different. I know you Michael; I know you so well. And so does she. You left the door open and she sat on the sofa reading or sketching, trying not to care.

I prepared your supper while you wrote to her — after you had read her latest letter. I used to prepare your supper and hate you and wonder how I ever got into this mess. Sometimes you would say, "How long before supper?" as you disappeared down the hall with Hester's letter in your hand. She wrote almost daily, but the letters tended to come in a bunch. We would stop at the Poste Restante — such a fancy name for the shoebox on the counter — and check to see if there were any letters. It was easy to recognize hers by the beautiful stamps. When you didn't get a letter, you worried. She was always with us in some way or another. "Hester says," you might begin, and then, with a fond smile on your face, read out some passage of description. Once you read out a bit where she said that although you would have arrived sooner or later at the point where you are now in your writing, living with me had been a kind of shortcut. I don't think that was the word, but it was a word like that. And you wondered why I threw a plate at you!

I sleep up on the roof now that it is getting really hot. Markos helped me drag one of the mattresses from your old study up here. It's lovely. If I were staying longer, I think I could make this roof another room. Get someone with a van or truck to take me to Réthimnon for big clay pots which I would fill with geraniums. Rugs or mats everywhere. Have a low table made. Would I turn into another Dog-Lady after a while? She is still here, by the way, but with a different dog. I finally spoke to her the other night. I was sitting at Zorba's sipping on ouzo and waiting for the Magic Boat to go out. There is a very strange thing that happens just at dusk. The white boat starts out, often with little boats behind it, and at one point it is as though the horizon simply raises itself, like a window, and there is a gap between earth and sky into which the boat suddenly disappears. I sit and watch it nearly every night now. It's lovely to come off the beach and sit at Takis' or Zorba's and sip ouzo and take my time, not have to worry about what I'm going to find you for supper.

Sometimes I go and get the mail and bring it back down to the square. No hurry; I have all the time in the world. I often eat out and then go for a walk. Last night, I had squid.

Sometimes when I come back, Markos and Heleni and the whole family are sitting outside on those ubiquitous straight-back chairs and chatting. Did you know there is no word in

17

Greek for "living room?" That's one of the things I learned in my course in Athens. "Tó living room:" that is how you say it. And one has only to look at the houses on this street to see why. How mad they must have thought us to want three rooms for two people. They probably thought we had seventeen relatives just out of sight around the corner, waiting until you and Markos had settled on a price.

They call to me and I join them. We discuss, in very simple sentences, the weather, the olives, Heleni's little garden, the woman at the end of the street who is about to have yet another baby. We sip wine or raki and soon Heleni disappears inside for a few minutes to reappear with pickled artichokes and cheese and melba toast. Markos often asks after you — I show him a letter with an African stamp. Heleni tells me he drinks too much, ever since the son left: it worries her. I look at photos of the grandchildren sitting on Santa's lap in some department store in Montréal. They ask to see the pictures of my girls again. Somehow the fact that I am a mother cancels out, or what? "respectablizes," the fact that I am living here alone and writing. Nevertheless I'm sure that I am an enigma (another good Greek word) to most of them. But they are very kind. Heleni comes up with a bouquet of flowers or cheese pies or some little treat nearly every day. "Eémaste ee athelphón," she told me the other day. "We are sisters."

You would never sleep up here on the roof, I wonder why? It was certainly warm enough when we arrived. Did you think someone might come up the stairs and murder us as we slept? In New York, you told me to walk closer to you, not because you feared for my safety, really, but your own. You said that you did not want to be put into a position where you might have to defend me and get hurt. That didn't seem ridiculous to me, just sensible. Yet sometimes you used Man as Defender as an excuse to get your own way. When you always wanted to sleep on the side of the bed nearest the door, back home. Or when you suggested that if we tried our ménage à trois down in Africa, it would be better for Hester to keep travelling as your wife, for that way she would have a "reason for being there." I was a published writer and therefore, presumably, "defined." And it was you, of course, who had no real reason for being there. Oh well, we all do it. I'm American-born, don't forget. I was taught early that one could rationalize what was politically expedient by declaring it morally correct.

But why wouldn't you sleep on the roof? You never really said. Did you somehow see that as too "romantic," once you had made up your mind to go back to Hester? Strange, how your siren song turned out to be security. "We were doomed," you write in this latest letter, "from the start." Perhaps we were. Given our natures and pasts, of course we were. I sometimes wonder if what you really wanted all along wasn't to keep Hester as your wife and me as your mistress on the side. The way, in fact, it was — for a brief while. Once, when I suggested that we go to her and tell her you said, "Hester would never stand for it." I accepted that. I didn't (then) want to break up your marriage and I didn't know you so well as I do now. Know how you use Hester (or her "feelings") as an excuse for doing what you want to do. "Hester wouldn't stand for it" translates as "I don't want to rock the boat, to have to make a choice." I've finally learned your language. "Hester sends her love."

There is a full moon tomorrow night. I have been taking a lot of notes on how the village looks at certain times of day, how it sounds. Do you remember the first night — and the donkeys? One would set off another, then another, then another. A great wheezing sound, like some very ancient machinery starting up, the Cosmic Engines perhaps, or statues calling out of throats of bronze. And then the dogs began to bark and the cocks began to crow and we lay in our beds, separated by a night table, and laughed and laughed. And I said, "Michael, may I come and crawl in bed with you?" I wasn't supposed to say that. The New Rules (unspoken but very real) were that now that you had re-committed yourself to your wife, I was supposed to wait for you to make advances. What *power* you had over me, that I could accept an arrangement like that! What power I gave you. I think that every time you fucked me you felt guilty, as though Hester were watching us from somewhere on the ceiling, like the cat in *Alice in Wonderland*. And I was always (towards the end) aware of this. But the first night in Aghia Sophia was like old times.

After she left you, the day you came to me in tears, we

went upstairs to my room and made love. Afterwards, you said to me, "I made love to Hester this morning — she asked me to — but I was thinking of you."

Did you think that was a compliment? Did you not think those words would come back to haunt me? (Much) later you wrote to me in Athens, declaring that we could remain deep friends, even though we could never be lovers again (And this time it was you I saw as the Cheshire Cat, me talking to you across a table at some distant date, and you, just a disembodied head floating a few inches above your soup plate). "It wasn't just sex, was it?" And then, perhaps because you still had some vague fantasy that things might work out for the three of us, you added, "Is it?" Oh my dear, it probably was just that. I was terribly lonely when I met you. I lived in a house full of friends and children and was admired and doing good work, but my body was very, very lonely. I had a couple of friends who were also sometimes lovers, but I needed to fall in love. And there you were. And there I was for you. You had been faithful to Hester for seven years; you were bored and restless. The ass is always greener on the other side. All our talk about "like minds" and the "wonders of deep conversation" was probably just a cover-up for the fact that our bodies cried out to one another. And probably still do. Physically, we are absolutely perfect mates and that's rare. "Just sex" can be a pretty big thing. It's all sexuality, isn't it? That's one of the things I'm learning. You, back with Hester, and relieved and happy to be once again in that safe harbour, were writing to me in Athens — or at least for the first little while. (Did Hester finally have it out with you? I hope so.) "I miss you. Think of you often — and not always as a 'mind' or even a 'fellow traveller.' I think of the dirty things I'd make you do, for example, if you were here. You know the ones I mean." And then you add, "But going on in this vein gives me an erection."

Once you wrote and asked me to pull down my panties and put my hand between my legs and think of you, imagine your fingers there. What was Hester doing when you wrote *that*? A manipulator is precisely that. Do you remember what I wrote back? I can't type so I don't have a copy, but it was some pun about "Dieu" and "Mon doigt" or

"Doigt de Seigneur," or something.

But that was in January. By the middle of February, discussing plans for a possible visit, you made it very clear that we could no longer sleep together. There would be no week in Kenya for the two of us alone. Border trouble, thieves wielding pangas. Couldn't leave Hester alone. People talk too much. But I must still come, you said. You were *both* looking forward to my coming. You had moved to a larger flat on the compound and could even put me up for a week or so in your study. We'd all take a ride on the Tan-Zan Railway. It sounded like a Chance card in Monopoly, and to continue the Monopoly metaphor, I knew I was back on Baltic Avenue again, with no houses and no hotels.

And finally, "I realize that if I want to stay married to Hester — and I do — that you and I cannot be lovers." You had tears in your eyes when you wrote that. It says so in the letter and I think I detect a little watermark just across the "l" so that lovers, on first reading, looks like "overs" or maybe even "ovens." It was hard to read, but I knew what it meant all right. And tonight's letter, nearly four months later, says you miss me. I'm sure you do. I'm just as big an egotist as you are and I know perfectly well how interesting I am. But the thing that interests *me*, the reason I'm sitting up here on this roof and writing, albeit the longest love letter in the world, is that, although I love you in some very real way, I do not miss you. You — or our relationship — got in my way. The intense electric glare of the first months, and then the long dark shadows of the last, kept me from seeing anything. And a writer writes with his eyes. Who said that? Gertrude Stein. It's true. We were never in Greece when we were down here together, or in Athens or Delphi or Meteora with Hester. That great lump, the Relationship, the PROB-LEM, blotted everything else out, some kind of awful eclipse of sensibility. I can't afford that kind of involvement.

To switch the image, I feel as though for two years I have been trying to fit into a dress that was both too small and not my style. Now I am back in my own comfortable clothes. I did the same to you, I suppose. Or I dressed you in clothes that were too big for you, that you weren't ready for, and then, was angry when you felt muffled and overwhelmed when you tripped. Your physical size deceived me. Let's put

21

it this way, Michael. I once had a distant relative of my grandfather's whom we used to drive out to the country and visit from time to time when I was a kid. She was almost totally deaf and used a black and silver ear trumpet, which was about the only thing I ever liked about the visit, because she'd let me and my sister try it. But she was senile and rambled on and on, getting everyone's name wrong and going back into what seemed to me, then, pre-history, and we would sit on the porch in our clean dresses and pick at the scabs on our knees and wait for her housekeeper to finally serve the lemonade. But, one day, she made a remark I'll never forget. An enormous dog, a sheepdog, I guess, came loping down the road and Aunt Aggie took a look at it and said in her high, cracked voice, "My, what a small dog in such a big box." We nearly wet our pants laughing.

How do you say "small man" in Swahili?

I knew you were married almost as soon as I met you. You gave me a story of yours which had appeared in a little magazine back East. In the credits, it said that you had a B.A. and were married. I thought, for some reason, that it sounded peculiar, but I guess it was because that sort of statement usually continues with "married and lives with his wife and two children and Samoyed 'Neige' in an abandoned railway car." Something clever like that. I saw you every Friday afternoon, first at the seminar, where I sat in as unofficial critic and, after that, over beer at the Graduate Centre. You knew that I was separated and had three children, but I see now that the FACT of my children, the full emotional weight of *that* statement, never hit you until you came to live with us. Friday afternoon was my one afternoon off. You knew me first without my children and fell in love with me that way. Your picture of me was distorted from the start. I think you saw me as always free to sit down and have a long talk about literature or life, as probably always free to retreat to the bedroom and make love. Your wife was your constant companion. Except when you both were at classes you did everything together — everything. Although you were always careful never to use each other's washcloth or towel. You told me that once after living with us for a few weeks. It was something we were very casual about and I was surprised. How much we are all creatures of (different) habit. I suppose I thought it symbolic of some kind of excessive tidiness in your marriage. I'm always analyzing things to death. You thought it awful that I would forget to put the cap back on the toothpaste. But we tried, both of us — or at first we did. I was going to be a better housekeeper and you were going to learn to cook. My daughters did not like you. They criticized your Shake 'n Bake chicken and asked why you put ketchup on your eggs. They thought you were loud and noisy and aggressive. You thought they were hostile little bitches. That was a year of tears and slammed doors. I don't just blame you, Michael, although I did at the time. I was on a plane just after you and I got together and the person sitting next to me was an extremely pretty young girl of about fourteen. She was rather nervous because she hadn't flown by herself before and was on her way to spend the summer with her father and his second wife. She talked pretty well non-stop. Her mother was a doctor, she said, and there were three children. Finally, I asked her if her mother had ever thought of marrying again. "No," she said immediately, and then, "Well, once." "What happened?" I said. She gave me a smile of such "professional innocence" (I can think of no other way to describe it) and then she said, in an offhand voice, "Oh, we put a stop to that." And suddenly, this sweet little teenager with her merry face and good manners was a character out of Henry James. That girl's words came back to me many times in the following months. So many things were happening at so many levels. First of all, you couldn't be their father because they have a perfectly good relationship with their father, whom they admire very much and with whom they live fifty percent of the time. Second of all, you just aren't "fatherly." Your first concern is yourself, always, and they weren't used to that — or to such an open admission of that. And then, you were too young to be a father to all but the youngest. So you related to them more or less as an older brother, which was fun for them sometimes (when you went to the movies or the Dairy Queen, or told them stories about your high school adventures and triumphs), but generally hard to take.

They'd never had an older brother. And when the older brother is also the mother's lover? Things get pretty complicated. And you had never experienced the divided attention that goes with being a parent. You told me several times, sitting on the edge of the bed, that you often found it very lonely living with me. "I love you, mind *and* body," you said once, "but Hester was a better companion." You admired my writing, but my writing times were somehow supposed to coincide with yours. You got up very early to write and by nine a.m., when I came back from taking my youngest daughter to school, you were ready for an extended coffee break, just when I was ready to begin. I was to adjust myself to you in every way. If I refused you said, half joking, "If you love me, why do you neglect me?" The children felt I neglected them for *you*. I felt as though I were being torn apart by all of you. I was never allowed any privacy or solitude. Sometimes I just wanted to shut the door of my room and crawl into bed alone. It was eleven p.m. I had been up since seven, being mother, writer, teacher, lover. When I told you this, you were hurt. "I can move out," you said, "I can move out anytime you say." Once, I fell asleep when we were beginning to make love. And yet I had never loved anyone, physically, the way that I loved you. When you touched me, my flesh smoked. That was the great power you had over me. For the first time in my life, I really understood the politics of male chauvinism, the conscious (or often unconscious) use of the power bestowed by genitals and the System.

In our ménage, Romance and Reality were always bumping heads. You began to take Hester out, regularly, on Tuesdays, "just for a swim and a chat." I suggested that on Tuesdays you spend the night in your study. You liked to make love to me on Tuesday afternoons. I was insanely jealous. Sometimes you wanted to make love to me again on Tuesday nights when you came home. I thought you were pretending I was Hester. I had been tutoring one or other of the children, or watching TV, or preparing for my students. And all the time, wondering what you and she were talking about, imagining her there, hair freshly washed; alert, supportive. And an excellent swimmer too. You began to compete to see who could do the most laps. She beat you every time. Laughing, you told me about it. That kind of competition was all right, no threat there. When she was part of an art exhibition, you cut an evening workshop to go to the opening; when I did a noon-hour reading, you said you were sorry, you couldn't come, you had to work right through lunch, you had so little time. And yet you would make love to me anytime. Sometimes, particularly on Tuesday nights, I saw you as a man with two separate bank accounts, both of which he wanted to keep open. Every Tuesday you put a few dollars in the Hester account, just to be on the safe side, but at that time the bulk of your investment went to me. Later, that whole business was reversed and yet you still want to keep a dollar or so with me. "I miss you." Remember this, remember that.

Remember the night you came out of your study back home and said, "Well, I know one thing. Whatever happens between you and me, I can never go back to Hester."

And I said, "It wouldn't be the same Hester you'd be going back to."

Heleni is milking her goat. I know the sounds of the street so well now that I do not even need to go to the edge of the roof and peer over. She will be standing in front of the grocery store, in her apron, facing the goat's rump, with the goat pressed tight against her. I can hear the milk hissing into the pail. Sss . . . sss . . . sss. The old man who mends saddles has just gone by on his donkey and greeted her, "Kalli-níck-tah, kalli-níck-tah." The slow velvet thuds of the little donkey's hooves never stop. The pregnant woman is calling in her children, "A-dón-ees, Ath-éh-nah." Do you remember how we laughed when we first came — the Hotel Acteon, the Acropol, the Ariadni Rent Rooms and down at the end of the street, the Hotel Ikaros, where the village priest sits on the balcony with his cronies (when he is not at the kaφenéon)? The other day, I heard a woman at the beach calling her little daughter, "APH-RO-DEE-TEE! APH-RO-DEE-TEE!" It's so wonderful. I feel that I am having a second chance at the village now, with you gone and our relationship resolved. All of my senses are peeled — not

25

just my eyes. I live in a kind of sensuous intoxication, like a honey bee in a field of flowers. I buzz — my whole soul buzzes — with impressions. Did I tell you that Heleni has painted our bedroom and my study and the passage up from the street a dusty pink? At first, I was horrified. It seemed a kind of cupcake pink, very hard to live with. Now I love it. It is like living in the heart of a pink sugar rose. But as the light changes, so does the colour, and the effect of coming in out of the glare of the street and up the white slab steps into all that pink is wonderful. I have a piece of bright cloth on the table in the bedroom and usually a bunch of daisies or geraniums, gifts from Heleni. The posters are gone, for I sent my trunk home from Athens, and the rugs, but it is still very pretty. I keep the shutters closed most of the day and I lie down in the hottest part of the afternoon. Last week, a strange wind blew up, very fierce and dry, as I imagine a wind from the Sahara might be, and the doors banged, and the shutters, and what wasn't banging was creaking. Like being on a ship in a storm. I had to prop the door open with stones and with the few books I have left. The wind's gone now, but Markos and Heleni say it will be back. Do you remember the storms in November, before I left? One begins to *feel* Homer, as well as see him. I say I do not miss you, but last week when the wind was here, twice I woke up crying. I cannot remember anything of the dreams which might have led up to this. I've given up my dream book for a while. Perhaps I wasn't crying about you at all.

After I challenged you in the Graduate Centre, you came to see me at the apartment of a friend whose fish I was minding in exchange for what I had planned as a precious weekend of quiet. I had earlier mentioned that I would be there over the weekend and suggested that you and Hester, who lived not too far away, in a student apartment, might like to drop over for a glass of wine. At that time, my friend Robert was absolutely crazy about tropical fish. I believe there were at least three aquariums bubbling away with all kinds of beautiful glowing little creatures moving in and out among the ferns. I have never possessed anything more grand than the traditional marmalade-coloured goldfish won at a fair or bought for a few cents at a pet shop. This, on the other hand, was a very classy set-up. Long aquariums, lit up and heat-controlled, tastefully furnished with the stones and seaweed appropriate to the habitat of the fish. I felt as though I were in a fish motel. I had put a record on the stereo and poured a glass of wine, and was intending to spend a quiet hour observing all the jewelled motion, when the buzzer rang. Your voice crackled up at me from eleven storeys below. I told you to come on up. I knew what I had said to you in the afternoon, but somehow I was not prepared for the sight of you, grim-faced and alone, your black umbrella dripping a large puddle outside the apartment door. I invited you in with a smile which you didn't return.

("What does O'Brien keep whispering in your ear?" one of the others had asked. We had been drinking beer for about two hours. "He keeps asking me when I am going to sleep with him," I said. The silence was immediate and intense.)

I sat on the sofa and you sat, jacket on, umbrella dripping between your legs, in an armchair opposite me. Maria Callas was singing something on the stereo. I noticed that you sat with your feet pointed slightly out, and how your legs were too long for your blue jeans. I thought how much you looked like Li'l Abner at that moment.

You cleared your throat.

"Can you take the record off?"

"I suppose so. I'm always afraid I'll scratch them if I turn them off in the middle. It's not mine."

You swallowed again.

"Well, I'd like you to turn it off; I have to talk to you."

And so, to the background bubbling of the three aquariums, it all came out. How what I had said that afternoon had not been fair to Hester. (Why didn't I kick you out right then, Michael, when you said that my remark had not been fair to Hester? Why?)

I replied that my remark had been prompted by a question concerning what *you* had said to me. *That*, somehow, was different. I had not played the game. Hester was very upset; you had gone home and told her what I'd done. She had cried. You had decided to come and have it out with me.

"Have *what* out??" My friend had pointed out certain fish

that could *not* be in the same aquarium with others. If I were a filmmaker or I wanted to make a film about our relationship, I think I would begin with those aquariums. Actually, our entire relationship has somehow been involved with water: walks in the rain, boat trips, the sea. Do you remember going around Manhattan on that day cruise? My agent had made us chicken sandwiches and we bought beer. As we passed Harlem, we learned what a Sugar Daddy was. That was a good day, no fights.

"Why you did what you did."

"I simply said out loud what you'd been saying for weeks. I'm sorry, I don't play games. I can never keep track of the rules. They're always different, you know. No two games alike."

"You were hardly being fair to Hester."

"Were you?"

Yet somehow, in the end, I was the one who was apologizing. I should not have spoken so in front of the other members of the seminar, all males, all (or all the ones who went on for beer) your friends. They all knew you were married; could see how awkward it was for you. What the hell was I apologizing for? I had called your bluff, that's all; but you looked so forlorn with your rain-soaked hair and your dripping umbrella and your wife crying herself to sleep back in your tiny apartment. So forlorn and so *innocent*, somehow. I took pity on you.

"I'm sorry if I caused trouble. I guess I was rather angry, in my heart, at what you were doing to me."

"?"

"Whispering sweet nothings in my ear, and you, a married man. I guess I wanted you to stop it." I told you, then, a little bit about the break-up of my own marriage. How I had to fight against a terrible cynical streak in myself, how I didn't trust men very much anymore.

You took off your jacket and accepted a glass of wine.

"I could never have a casual affair with someone like you," I said. "You're too serious and so am I. It wouldn't work."

You nodded and smiled your beautiful smile (I had solved the whole thing) and we were friends again. I was just going to suggest that perhaps you should go and get your wife when the buzzer buzzed for the second time that evening and my current boyfriend arrived. I told you quickly and briefly about him, how we were very good friends and only incidentally lovers (and I said I didn't play games!). Then I showed you out, after introducing the two of you at the door. I walked to the elevator with you.

"I'm glad we had this chat."

"I'm glad too."

Then, just as the door opened and you went to step in, I made my fatal mistake.

"Let's kiss and make up," I said, lifting my face towards yours. You held the door open with one hand and bent over me.

Our stunned faces stared at each other as the door slid shut.

"All Cretans are liars." I remember this as a problem from some far-off course in philosophy or logic. It is said by a Cretan and, therefore, what do you do? An irresolvable problem. Here is another one:

I HATE YOU
I LOVE YOU

EVERYTHING ABOVE THIS
LINE IS TRUE

It's all so bloody complicated, isn't it?

During the winds last week, I had a vision of the sky as a piece of fabric and imagined waking up in the morning with the heavens hanging down in torn blue shreds. Instead, there was Heleni up on the roof trying to anchor the wild sheets to the line. I tried to help her and we both ended up getting slapped in the face with sopping cloth. We giggled like schoolgirls and, later, I sat in her kitchen, which is also her dining room and bedroom, looking at photos of her son in Canada and eating rice pudding made with hot goat's milk.

29

Two fat neighbour babies lay sleeping on the bed. Reluctantly, I returned to my writing for a while and then went down and sat in the street with all the ladies. They offer me so much — tea, pop, cheese pies, friendliness — and I come empty-handed. Sometimes I hold the wool while Heleni's mother winds it, or buy a watermelon which we all share.

The book I am working on now is about you and me (of course) — or it started out that way. I began it in an attempt to discover how I could have violated my own moral code (there's the American in me again) in that particular way. But there's Crete and this village and this street and all that seems much more interesting than the story of how I fell in love with you and all the complications of the affair. Sometimes I feel like one of those Impressionist painters who cheerfully sacrificed the subject, as subject, to a study of the changing effects of light. Lovers in a landscape, perhaps, but the lovers are just part of the landscape — they are shape, tone, movement (or lack of it), not STORY. The trees and rocks are just as important. I want to stop looking for the "eternal aspect" of the story, although it's probably harder here than anywhere else in the world, where hotels are named Ikaros and little girls "APH-RO-DEE-TEE." The whole fucking island is "charged." How to capture the island and leave the myth alone — it's difficult. I want to capture the sound of Heleni's loom or the sunlight on that white wall over there or the moment when the Magic Boat goes through that gap in the horizon. And so, I put my pen down and lay a big rock on the pages I have written so far (not many) and join the ladies, or go swimming, or climb the hill. I blink when I step out into the sunlight. "Kalli-máre-a, kalli-máre-a." The blonde woman comes out of her house and puts my hand on her enormous belly so that I can feel the baby kick. Someone is drying octopus on a clothesline in front of the house.

The grapevine along the balcony outside your study is lush now and two doves come regularly to sit there. "Perdue," they seem to say, "per-doo-oo-oo." I do not go over to that side to be closer to *you*, to sit on the chair you sat at, typing away, reciting your novel out loud so that I could hear you through the tiny toilet window, but to observe the road which screws down into the village. The tourists have begun to arrive — motorbikes with girls hanging on in back, cars, vans. The five-thirty bus from Herakleion, the one that brings the mail, is nearly always full. They get out, get their packs down off the roof, mill about the square, climb the steps up to some of the "Rent Rooms" signs beyond. Lots and lots of Germans — to me, this is both strange and sad. Presumably, their fathers told them how beautiful it was. How do the Cretans really feel about that? The widows? The old men who sit at the kaφenéon. When they hear the language, do they shudder or do they just accept? ENIK ·ΔΩΜ·, some of the hand-lettered signs say. The Greek abbreviation for "Rent Rooms." Then (often), underneath, "Zimmer Frei." German is the first language they try on you if they see you are European. In Athens, at the wine merchant's, even after I had learned my social Greek, the old man would look up from the shadow of his huge barrels and reply to my "kallimera" with "Guten Tag, Fräulein." And count out the money for me in German. It gave me the creeps. His wife (or possibly daughter) was an idiot. She sat in a corner hugging herself and rocking back and forth. I held out my bottles; one for cheap retsina, one for ouzo. "Epharistó," I would say, "Epharistó polée." "Danke," he would say, fitting the bottles into my basket. "Auf Wiedersehen."

The widows stand out so clearly here in this white-walled village. Punctuation marks. Reminders of mortality. How many were widowed by the Germans? Now the young men and women lie on the beach in their skimpy bathing suits and after a few days they are golden brown. Youth, the master race. The other day, I thought how much they looked like athletic trophies: tall, long-legged, golden. The Deutsche Mark is very strong these days; it is welcome everywhere. Yet when the quail whistle at night, I think of German sentries signalling to one another and wonder if the old widows ever hear that sound and tremble.

We sat in the Hong Kong Kitchen with the rain streaming down outside and the windows misted over. In an hour the children would be home from visiting their father and I would have to go back to the house. I had spent the weekend watching the fish, reading, listening to music, sleeping a lot. Sleep, I suppose, is my way of escaping. But I like lying down generally — The Horizontal Woman. I used to tell my husband that my great dream in life was to lie in bed all day eating chocolates and reading love magazines. It was a joke between us. To all outward appearances, I am exactly the opposite sort of woman. Now that interviewers have begun to interview me one of the standard questions seems to be: "How did you manage to do all you did and still have young children about?" One of my standard replies, which must make my ex-husband laugh, if he ever reads those things, is: "Well, I didn't do it by lying in bed all day eating chocolates and reading love magazines." But there is a lazy, indolent, sluttish core in me somewhere — it's more than just a question of escape.

The rain never let up and a perfect wall of rain poured down outside the apartment window. I felt safe and protected and cut off from all responsibility — except the fish, of course. (I had been warned about temperature control and the dangers of too much powdered shrimp.) The noise of the rain outside and the gurgling of the aquariums within, plus my own fatigue, held me in a kind of suspension, like one of those little Cartesian men in a bottle, and this was quite rare and wonderful. My boyfriend? my lover? had left in the wee hours of Saturday morning — he never spent an entire night with me unless I stayed over at his place — and since then, I had seen only the fish and one bedraggled seagull who had used the balcony railing as a rest stop. The phone was off the hook. I had never lived in an apartment so that in itself was a new experience. They had always seemed to me cold, sterile, impersonal (and with children, out of the question). Now I could see the attraction.

From time to time, I wondered idly what it would have been like to make love with you. I thought that you were a nut — and could not really imagine why you had told your wife what I had revealed in the Graduate Centre, unless: 1) It boosted your ego in some strange way, or 2) You were terrified that someone else would tell her, or mention it in front of her. But that kiss had shaken me a bit — like striking a single match and getting a minor explosion. You were —

you are — an extraordinarily good-looking man. When I first noticed the resemblance of your head to that of the Poseidon of Artemision, that was not a starry-eyed bit of nonsense. The resemblance is quite remarkable, as you yourself saw. The long, straight nose, the full, sensual mouth, the magnificent hair and beard: it is all there. His legs are better than yours, and his torso, but then, he doesn't suffer from a slight curvature of the spine and anyway, he's a god. There is a fish boat down in the bay just now: ΠΟΣΕΙΔΩΝ. How I should love to have a photo of you beside it. Or maybe not. I seem to have a plethora of photos of you as it is. You don't look Canadian, Michael — you are too tall and too black and your skin is too dark. Perhaps some pirate slipped off a ship and surprised your great great great great grandma as she bent over picking flowers in a field. You come from a warmer, sunnier clime. (Hence, our delight in the photo I took in Latakia. You leaning against the ship's rail in that kufiyya and agal, the Arab headdress, with all those freighters in the distance and the intense blue sky above. Sheik Michael on his private yacht. The perfect A-Rab, as the Chief Engineer said when he came around the corner of the deck and saw me posing you.)

So — I had always, even before the kiss at the elevator, found you an attractive man, but as I generally don't fancy husbands, I had never fantasized about you or even entertained the notion of sleeping with you. Or not consciously. A couple of the other fellows, yes, but not you. Looking back now, I wonder why I called your bluff that day, why I brought it out in the open. Of course now I know that you had been fantasizing about me, even thinking about me when you masturbated, although you said that you could never actually imagine what IT would be like.

You were soon to find out, however.

On Sunday, the buzzer startled me — I was expecting no one. It was you again, wanting to come up, wanting to know if I was alone. Yes, I said, but getting ready to go home. I'd promised to be back by half past four. You had to talk to me, you said. Come on up then, I said, but you can't stay very long.

So there you were again, even wetter than before, if that were possible, and certainly more miserable. You had spent

33

a terrible weekend, you said. You realized that you were powerfully attracted to me and you didn't know what to do about it. I suggested that I get my stuff together and we go out for a cup of tea. It seemed to me a good idea to talk in some public place. I did not exactly think you would make a scene — I just thought we would be better out of that small apartment with Robert and his girlfriend due any minute and the bedroom on view from the little hallway, where you were standing dripping, looking as though you were about to burst into tears.

We went to the Hong Kong Kitchen and while people all around stuffed their faces with garlic shrimp and Wun-tun soup or whatever, we sat in a corner by the window and talked. Your black umbrella lay like a drowned crow on the floor by our feet. I told you I really had to get back home. I told you a little about the break-up of my marriage and how perhaps there were moments in everyone's life when the grass on the other side was an almost overpowering green. I told you again that you were not the type of man that I felt I could have a casual affair with, for my own sake, if not for yours. You said you couldn't sleep and stared at the misted window, blinking back the tears. All this time, the little Chinese girl behind the counter was calling out numbers.

"Thirty-eight," she said.

"That's how old I am," I said. "I'm not a young girl. I have three children and my life is already pretty complicated." Your long, fine-fingered hand (you win over Poseidon as far as hands go — you have the most beautiful hands I've ever seen) lay on the table and I took it.

"I think you're lovely," you said.

At that point, I should have got up and left. What good was reason at that stage? But no one had called me "lovely" in a long, long time. A big tear was rolling down your cheek.

"I'm new. I'm different. We're both writers and so have a common obsession. I'm not lovely. I get tired and cranky and my figure went long ago and I have a terrible time balancing all the demands made on me and I snore if I sleep on my left side."

You buried your head in your arms.

"Don't," I said, "or I will start to cry. Do you think I

want to put myself down? If you weren't married, it would be different. But you are." I gathered up my things. The Good Woman Sadly Walks Away. "We never got our tea. Never mind. I'm going to take the bus just up the way. Come and walk me to the bus stop."

You nodded and blew your nose. I thought how lovely your eyes were, even full of tears. Later, I said that your eyes reminded me of the trout streams I used to go to with my father as a child. A rich dappled green and brown. But slightly slanted, like the eyes of an animal, not a man: wolf's eyes. Hester told me once that she fell in love with you for your eyes.

(And if you had not kissed me on the eyelids one night, Michael, when you had come to bed late and thought that I was sleeping, if you had not kissed me on the eyelids and whispered, "Goodnight, my love," all this would be so much easier. For you are not just sweet Michael in tears in the Hong Kong Kitchen telling me I'm lovely and all that shit, you are also Michael the egotist, the liar, the hypocrite, the coward, the man who asked me, when I took your letters and cards along with mine to the steward to be mailed at some port or other, "How many ideas did you steal off my postcards?" the man who referred to me over and over again as "that fucking bitch.")

Dog-Lady (Dog-Girl, she should be called, as she really can't be more than twenty-five or twenty-six) told me that she had one hundred potted plants and sixteen canaries. She said she had been sick. A real Greek, as far as the canaries go. Nearly every balcony in Athens has at least one cage hanging from it. I hate the idea of caged birds and it really surprised me to hear Dog-Girl refer to her canaries. I had seen her as another "free spirit," not quite a Matala type, but definitely not someone you would think was "into" caged birds. She still wears the same little faded sundress, like a child's dress, over her bathing suit and begs scraps for her animal from the people eating in the narrow street of the tavernas. Do you remember the night we saw her dancing with her dog? Her new dog is much smaller. She speaks to it in Greek. Yannis (at Zorba's Bar) says she is a whore, πουτανα (poo-tana). That's how she supports herself. I don't know. Certainly her Greek is fluent and she seems to know all the fishermen. Yet I do not know that this village is sophisticated enough yet to allow a foreign whore to set herself up and sleep with its men. I'd like to ask Heleni, but my Greek isn't good enough and I've never seen her down on the square, although her old father, the fisherman, sits under a tree on the far side, somewhat apart from the tourists, and drinks in the afternoons with all his cronies.

Would Dog-Girl and I become friends if I stayed here, I wonder? I spoke to her the other night and her answers were polite, but fairly abrupt. I asked her dog's name by way of openers. "Spiro." Not very original, I thought. I have never seen her talking to another woman — always to the men — so perhaps the whore story is true. Perhaps the fishermen come quietly at night to her green and singing rooftop over the taverna. One by one. Tucking their coarse shirts into their pants as they go quietly back down the stairs in the moonlight. Would they pay her in fish, in squid, in baskets of shining eels? What would it be like to lie in the arms of one of those brown, muscled men? There is one who is repairing his boat just now, down on the beach right next to Zorba's Bar. He smiles at me sometimes and I smile back or say, "The weather is fine" or "The sea is calm." Είναι γαλήνη remarks like that. But I am too shy to carry it further. And this afternoon, I noticed one of the German girls was helping him scrape the keel. She probably just walked right over in her white bikini and picked up the scraper. As a sexual adventuress, I am a dead loss in reality, but I can imagine those rough hands moving over my body and that curly head on my shoulder. It's got nothing to do with age; I couldn't have picked up his scraper at twenty-one, lean and flat-bellied as I was then. You are the only man in the world who has ever seen me as sexually provocative, and that, in relation to other men. Hester said you were simply projecting your own fantasies onto others, I don't know. You were always telling me to button up my blouse. Once you even suggested I should wear a bra. I am small-breasted; I don't need a bra. If I needed one, I assure you I would wear one — out of vanity, if nothing else. Hester wears one. I wonder if you asked her to. She doesn't need one either.

In Latakia, I put my hand on the shoulder of a sailor who was steadying me as I climbed to the bow of the tender, getting ready to jump onto the ladder of the freighter. I was terrified and it had not occurred to you to offer to help me. The sea was choppy and I had visions of myself missing the jump and being instantly crushed between the small boat and the big. He offered me his shoulder to hang onto. Afterwards, you said that I had been "indiscreet" and probably had made a fool of you in front of all the other men in the tender (crew from other freighters, two Greek engineers, three itinerant traders). I told you I had been afraid. You, with your long legs and athlete's body, stopped your tirade in mid-sentence.

"Afraid of *what*?" you said.

I explained.

"A little jump like that!"

(In Aghia Sophia, in our makeshift flat over the grocery store, we made a rule that after our halt for breakfast we would retreat to our respective studies until lunch. No interruptions for any reason whatsoever. "Yes, yes," I agreed, "that's the way it must be!" So I was surprised when you knocked on my door. Where were the band-aids, you said. You knew perfectly well where they were, I said, annoyed at this break in my routine. The novel was not going well. The fact of your leaving kept getting in the way. The last thing I needed was your head poking around the door and enquiring after band-aids.

"I've cut myself," you said.

"I assumed that," I said, turning my back on you and pretending to take up my work again.

But I couldn't keep it up. I went and got the band-aids and fixed your finger.

"You call that a cut?" I said.

"I wanted a hug," you said.

But if I had ever done that to you?)

Once you said to me, "You and I would probably get on perfectly well if we had servants." Heleni thought it was wonderful that you cooked spaghetti every Friday night. Markos, I feel, never really believed it. And I shall tell you something really wonderful, Michael, something you would otherwise never know, because you would never sleep up on the roof, and because, in so many ways, you never lived here at all — or only in your study and perhaps in the post office at five-thirty p.m., waiting for another letter from Africa. Well, this is it. This is what I have discovered: THE PRIEST'S MOTHER RINGS THE BELLS. I saw her last Sunday morning climbing down from the little tower. I had my glasses with me because I was taking notes about the way the morning spreads down over the hill across the way, coats the hill with honey-coloured light, finally hits the houses. I heard the bells begin the ring. DA DA DAH DA DA DAH DA DA DA DA DA DA DAH. No wonder they always sound so angry! More like an alarum signal than any call to worship. I peered down the street and there she was, coming backwards down the ladder. I suppose *he* was still asleep or sipping coffee. What a nice life! I see him at the καφενέον next to the grocery store where we used to go — where I still go for the things I can't get from Markos and Heleni — or sitting on the balcony of the Hotel Ikaros talking talking talking. One night I saw him, or the back of him, leaning in the window down the street, watching a television show. And his mother rings the bells! Is he celibate — I mean, *really*? I met two men in Athens. One was an importer and the other was just finishing up a commission in the army. They were cousins. The army officer was twenty-nine and still a virgin. Until he went in the army, he had slept in the same room as his mother. I had to cough into my hand to keep from laughing. The other one (older; separated from his wife, but not divorced) confessed that *he* had slept in the same bed with his mother, his arms around her breasts, until he was twenty-one! The mothers are very powerful here and their greatest joy is their sons. Perhaps the priest's mother is the most powerful woman in the village. Perhaps they sleep in the same bed. I have a feeling that they actually *own* the Hotel Ikaros and the old man, the one who introduced us to Markos and Heleni, simply manages it for them.

What does the priest think of all the bare flesh — for *he* goes down to the square, especially on Sunday afternoons when families come from as far away as Réthimnon to bathe in the sea and to sit underneath the awnings of the tavernas, eating plates of shrimp. I have seen him at the head of a long table, stuffing his face and talking in his loud, rather abrupt way. I have watched his eyes over the napkin, have seen them follow the movement of a golden thigh. Does he get huge erections under those long black skirts? He is handsome and in his prime, maybe fifty-five, no older. He peels his shrimp carefully and wipes his plate thoroughly with a piece of bread. Doesn't he fuck at all? No one? Has he never? There was a bishop in a town near here who was famous for *his* amours. Apparently he especially liked young widows and the phrase was that he "liked to get them while they were still warm." Yannis told me that story, but when I asked him about the priest, he shut up and got very uneasy, even though he is not a local boy. Yannis has trouble with *his* mother. She may sweep up in front of his bar while he is still sleeping it off upstairs, but she really rules the place. He has an English girlfriend, quite new, and the old mother is very jealous. The other night she threw a tin of olive oil at the girl as she was helping out behind the bar. It missed her and hit the wall with a terrible thud. Ah yes, the mothers. Quite rightly to be feared.

"You aren't a good wife to me," you said.

And I, exasperated, asked, "Well, what's your definition of a good wife then?"

"A wife is someone who is always there when you need her."

"No," I said, "that's the mother of a child under five."

You wanted me to be your *soror mystica*, your mystical sister, who would talk art all day and make love all night and miraculously still find time to do the housework and cook your dinners. And in return, what were you offering? Your presence; your *definition*, as it were. That was to be your gift. The old cock and bull story.

"Don't you find it nice to have a man around the house again?" you said to me one day. Just to "have" one around the house! Incredible. The fact that I defined myself in other ways at first irritated and then overwhelmed you. "It's nice to have *you* around," I said.

Later you could be quite philosophical about it. "In my life, you are absolutely unique," you wrote, "without parallel. You are not only the most magnificent woman I have ever known, you are the most magnificent person. That, I suppose, is close to the crux of the matter and has to do with one of the many many things you taught me about yourself. *I* have to be the most magnificent creature around. Not very nice — and not very nice from a number of perspectives to say — but there it is. I can't be with you, Rachel, because you're too fucking great."

And then you add, you *add*, in parenthesis:

"(That's your cross, Rachel. You can only grin and bear it.)"

My *cross*!

I sat with that letter in my hands and I laughed and laughed until I cried. What arrogance! What presumption! That my greatness should be my "cross." And yet, of course, you are right. Women are supposed to define themselves through the men they love: wife of the Prime Minister, mother of the priest. Wife of the rising young novelist. How you hated it if we went to a party or gathering of some sort and I got more attention than you. I began to apologize (to you), to turn down invitations to do readings. (If I went out of town, you would pick up the phone and call Hester, take her to a show. She began to become, for me, "the other woman." And over that tumultuous year, I began to visualize your ego as a very large dog to which you were irrevocably chained, which was constantly hungry. And Hester was the one who was always there with the Gravy Train, even before the dog began to whimper.)

"If you love me, why do you neglect me?"

Oh Michael, Michael, how can I blame you? I wasn't born male in a society where men lead and women follow. And you were always so concerned with what people might think or say. It wasn't enough that I loved you mind *and* body, that I brought you the secrets of my heart (a heart which, because of you, was allowed or enabled to thaw out from the ice-pack into which I had thrust it). It wasn't enough that I had truly and willingly committed myself to you. "As much of myself as I could to anyone," I said. And for you, that last admission cancelled out all which had gone before.

We slept in one another's arms after evenings which often began late with you and me sitting up in bed with a bottle of wine talking talking talking, and then the lovemaking just an extension of the talk, so that sometimes it was hard to tell which was which, whole paragraphs of touch punctuated by kisses. I had never felt so free with anyone before. You loved my head between your thighs, would push up against my cheek, your long fingers twisting in my hair; I loved you tasting me, touching me, moving up to enter me and laying your dark head, with a sigh, upon my shoulder. "Hello, love," you would say, your eyes full of tears, "hello, my love." Or — naughty — I would clamp my legs together or keep my panties on until you forced them down and off me and forced my legs apart, tickling me until I yielded. One of the girls might come in the next morning. "This room stinks of sweat."

(Do you remember the hotel in New York, Michael? The mirrors? You sitting naked in the pale blue velvet chair and me kneeling on the rug in front of you.)

Maybe the next day we would have a fight because it was your turn to clean the bathroom. We all had jobs in the house — you, me, the girls — everyone. I would scream at you, "Even geniuses sometimes clean bathrooms," and you would storm down the stairs and out the front door yelling, "Fucking bitch, you fucking bitch." Neither would give an inch. Awkward apologies would (eventually) be made. Each wanted what we had before and the new thing as well.

The children did not help. You scared them with your shouting. Their father is not a shouter and shows his stubborness in other ways. And if they looked scared, then I became Mother Hen, Mother Bear, Mother Lioness. Some of their criticisms of you were valid. Some were made simply to annoy. "Didn't you ever cook *anything* before? Who was your servant last year?" (And we all knew who. That one usually led to the slamming of the front door.)

But they liked you at first — when you were just a friend of mine, one of the writers from the seminar — and not my lover. Were they also angered by our sexuality — or mine? It is quite possible. In a strange way, parents are not supposed to be sexual creatures; that idea is very threatening.

And for three years, they had me to themselves. All the men I went around with (and there weren't many), I had known from my married days. You were the new ingredient. Even their father's girlfriend was an old friend of ours.

And you had Hester all to yourself.

Do you know what you wanted, Michael, what maybe you still want? Someone loyal and helpful to whom you can dedicate your books: "To Hester, without whose loving help . . ." "To my wife," or simply, "Once again, to Hester." Someone to whom you could look back on in old age (for I'm sure you would outlive that kind of woman) and say, with tears in your eyes, "There's no other word for it − she was a saint." Hester is so deprecatory about her own art − "Oh, *that*. I never see myself as an artist." − whereas you overpraise her to such an extent that it's embarrassing to hear. And so the agreed-upon game goes on. Or does it? Somehow I think you are in for horrible times with Hester. You are not quite so perfect in her eyes as once you were. I doubt if she'll be as dependent on you as before.

The other day, I was swimming, Michael, with the mask and snorkel that you gave me and taught me how to use. There was a slight wind and the sunlight coming down through the water made a pattern on the ocean floor like a golden net. The sea and I, the swimmer, could have been gathered up in that net, along with the little opalescent fish who crossed so close in front of my eyes. I could hear my breath − in/out, in/out − and I felt so calm, so at peace, so utterly content. Do you remember how afraid I was to use the mask the first time, how I was afraid I wouldn't be able to breathe? You were very patient with me sometimes, with my fears. You were a good teacher. Do you think, if I had been anything but a writer, it might have worked? Hester's painting doesn't bother you at all. Although perhaps it would if she were to become known before you do. Anyway, I doubt that she ever paints right through the hour when it is time to cook dinner. I once met the wife of a well-known English potter. She was a painter, and quite a good one too. In the kitchen, there was an oven-timer, not the kind attached to the oven, but separate, portable. She sometimes used it to time things on the stove, but its primary function was to be with her in her studio in case she got "carried away" and forgot to start the lunch or dinner. She wound it up an hour before she had to quit. Well, he supported her by teaching as well as making pots — it was an "arrangement." You and Hester have taken turns supporting one another and have both worked at the same time, pooling your money. It's an aspect of "women's liberation" that you heartily endorse. And yet you still want/need the traditional roles: Man of the House and Little Woman. Underneath the blue jeans and beard, I see a nineteenth century gentleman, perhaps a bank clerk in a stiff collar, who is determined to lead a very structured life. Well, it's easier if the artist makes that kind of arrangement — everything's settled and then he can get on with the "real" business of his life. Maybe I'm just jealous because I don't have a wife like yours. What I think has been the hardest thing for me to get through my head is that you have not chosen between two *individuals*, each of whom you love, but between two ways of life and two ways of relating to a woman. You tried the conventional way and, obviously, found it dissatisfying — at that time — so you found me. But you are still too self-centred and weak-egoed to ever be able to make it with someone who insists on mutuality. So, for a while, last fall, you wanted both *modes*, not both people, and the idea of the ménage à trois was your refusal to acknowledge this or take responsibility for it, as well as our refusal, Hester's and mine, to insist that you grow up. You know how children can manipulate a situation between competing adults — and you were just like a child; you *are* a child — and the dynamics were identical. One of the things Hester said during our big blow-up in Athens was that she guessed she loved you the way I loved my children and I yelled at her, "But he's about to be thirty years old!" The way you love an adult is *not* the way you love a child and, for the first time, in the midst of my anger and frustration and tears, I was afraid for you, afraid of Hester's "love." But instead of being aghast at such a terrible admission, you turned on me. And then it was all over, as they say, but for the shouting.

That raw octopus drying on the clothesline, those great skeins of blue-dyed wool. I love this street. I love it. It will be very hard to go back to a city where nearly everything takes place inside. My teacher in Athens says the Greeks have no traditional word for "blue." Is that possible? I will have to find a Greek scholar and ask. Certainly the word she gave us, "bleu," is not Greek. It cannot be declined and, therefore, is foreign. Maybe that's why Homer kept calling it the wine-dark sea. Heleni is frying fish in olive oil; I can smell it. If I went down, she would ask me to join them. It's very tempting. Markos would draw off some of that strong wine of his and I could practice my Greek. (But tonight I will pass that up, barbouni and wine and chat. I am dedicating tonight to you.)

"We changed each other," you write, "it seems to me. Or through each other, we found out things about ourselves." Yes, that's more like it — we found out things about ourselves. I realized how many things about myself I could *not* change, how many doors I had gone through and closed behind me forever. I learned that I, who saw myself as weak, am really very strong. I learned that I could love someone and hate him at the same time and this has led me to ponder the whole nature of what we call "love." Sometimes I think I fell in love with you because I was at last ready to fall in love again and you just happened along. Like taking any streetcar or hailing an expensive cab when you're tired and have been waiting a long, long time. Just to get going, to get moving. Sometimes I think the very thing I hate in you, your egotism, was what I fell in love with. There is enormous energy involved in egotism. Perhaps I fell in love with that energy. Then, of course, there was all the delicious erotic tension of a moral dilemma — the letters vowing that we would never, could never, see one another again. Letters which, more often than not, were delivered by (trembling) hand.

So there would be the letter saying, "I mustn't see you anymore" and then the "I" would be in the coffee shop where we had agreed to meet. Some say that the maze of Knossos was only a dance, and a ritual dance at that. Was that what we were doing, the oldest dance in the world?

Do you remember the first time we made love? (I'm sure

44

you do.) It was almost as though you were a sexual gymnast, showing me everything you could do. Your body was covered in sweat and I was rather frightened. I felt lust, not love, coming from you to me. And yet, I suddenly reached up my arms and whispered, "Michael, I love you." It was a lie when I said it and yet as soon as I said it, it was true. Like the kiss at the elevator, my declaration to you came as a surprise and left me shaken. Left you shaken as well. Later, you told me that you had not been able to come until I said that.

We lay quiet together for a while. Your heart thudded like the sound of hoofbeats against my ear.

Then you got dressed, went downstairs and went out the door.

Went home and told your wife what we had done.

I have made up a new verb, Michael — "pedestal-ize." Maybe it popped into my head because of the months in Athens. All those museums and all those Sundays on the Acropolis in the presence of the Caryatids, both real and fake. (Although the great glory of archaic and classical sculpture seems to have been the male figure, there are quite a few stone ladies or goddesses around as well.) Anyway, you pedestalized me, my dear, as all Romantics do to their women, and so there was no place to go but down. I kept telling you I had feet of clay, but you wouldn't listen. You believed in "the marriage of true minds" and forgot that that guy also wrote "My mistress' eyes are nothing like the sun." When enlightenment came (which always occurs when two people actually live together), you were terribly disappointed. Hester who, because of familiarity, had been knocked off her pedestal, was quickly put back on. A little chipped and cracked perhaps, a toe or two missing, but that just added to poignancy, like that row of sometimes headless, sometimes armless sculptures we saw at the Forum in Rome. (Do you remember the one which was only a toga-wrapped lap and legs, seated on a bench?) You began to extol the virtues of the woman you had turned your back on: her kindness, her integrity, her loyalty, what a good companion she had been. Now all of these things are true; but, if you had deliberately

45

set out to make me hate her, you couldn't have done a better job. And you did not hesitate to point out to me that she would never have done what I had done, gone to bed with a happily married man.

I fell for it all. You sowed seeds of jealousy and anger in me, but especially seeds of guilt. Lying in your arms, half-asleep and content, I would suddenly imagine Hester in her room in the communal house where she now lived, weeping silently into her pillow (so that no one would hear) and wondering where she had failed. Then I hated you for loving me and I would lie awake long after you had fallen into a smiling post-coital sleep. For I had been a Hester too and I knew what it was to be left, and to lie alone.

"Why don't you go back to her then?" I would sometimes cry.

"Because I love *you*."

"Why, since you think I'm so awful?"

"Because I do."

(Did you know the Greek word for "why" and "because" is the same?)

You tapped away at me, Michael, with your little hammer and chisel, tap tap tap, and eventually, you knocked me off my pedestal completely. I suppose I should be grateful; I'm a woman, not a goddess (although at times you saw a parallel between you and me and Calypso and Odysseus; and Hester mentioned that she saw us *both* as gods!) and I was spending too much of my energy trying to live up to *your* ideal, not mine. Hester really *is* a nicer person, although she constantly denies it; it's easier for her to be nice.

And maybe she is right. Maybe she doesn't have any talent, or only a pinch — not enough to dedicate her life to art. I don't know. It's not my field so it's hard for me to tell. The paintings she did during her year alone were terrible anguished cries. I went to that student exhibition (She had invited *all* of us, even the girls) and thought, "Yes, the pain is there and very real, but where is the organization?" She is at the beginning of a long, long road and who could blame her if she turned back and decided to walk along behind you instead. You are so obviously talented, so (already) dedicated. It is easier and probably more rewarding to be the wife of an artist than to be the artist herself. She is *not*

sure and one has to be sure in order to develop the selfish-
ness necessary to pursue one's art, whatever happens. Women
are not brought up to be *that* kind of selfish. Like the moon,
our symbol, we are supposed to bask in reflected light. To
walk in someone else's shadow is light enough. ("I can't be
with you because you are too fucking great. That's your
cross, Rachel, and you'll just have to grin and bear it." Or
Virginia Woolf: "*Anon* was probably a woman.")

And I'm a Romantic too, Michael. I idealized you as well.
Then, in February, cynical Robert wrote: "So in the cold
light of dawn, the Prince turned out to be only a frog after
all."

The moon will be up soon. It's fun to sit in the square, at
Yannis' bar, and watch how quickly it comes up over the
hill. And how clear the stars are here. I would like to know
their names; particularly here in Greece, I would like to know
their names. All those people and creatures tossed up into the
sky for reward or punishment. On the freighter, they still
chose, on clear nights, to navigate by the stars; the windows
of the saloon and the crew's quarters were blacked out. We
used to stand side by side and look up at the sky, the moon
bouncing slightly because of the motion of the ship. I usually
went down to the cabin first and you stayed on deck a little
longer. I knew that was probably time you spent fantasizing
about Hester, but there wasn't much I could do about it. We
would be standing with our bodies touching, and yet suddenly, I would feel you move away from me — mentally,
I mean. That's when I would usually say, "Well, I guess I'll
go down now."

Some nights you played poker with the steward and the
Chief Engineer and some of the fellows from the crew. I had
agreed to back you if you lost, if you would split your
winnings. You hardly ever lost. The crew taught you to say,
in Norwegian, "Astrid, show me your cunt." Astrid being
the shy one, the less pretty chambermaid; of course, she
would be the one they would pick on. You thought it was
very funny, and if Astrid served us at the table, you would

look at me with a little smile. I think by the end of the trip you had won over $400.00. Anyway, we split it.

They all knew we weren't married, even though the passenger list said we were: Mr. and Mrs. Michael O'Brien, Montréal, Canada. We had used our separate names when we booked the tickets, but somehow the company had lumped us together as a married couple. Maybe there was some archaic rule about sharing a cabin or something. You were very upset when they sent you the tickets in Montréal. You mentioned it in one of your lying (collect) phone calls. Perhaps Hester had been with you when they came? You had them sent to your parents. Perhaps you just felt it "wasn't fair to Hester" — a phrase I had heard all too often. Poor thing. There *she* was going down to Africa by herself (and on a long and boring plane ride) and there you were, setting sail (so to speak) on a month long freighter trip with a woman purporting to be your wife. You felt *guilty*, Michael, didn't you, even though it was all out in the open by this time that you were going down (across?) to join her, your "real" wife, after Christmas? Why did she ever agree to that freighter trip? Was it because she knew how much you wanted it (the tickets were bought, after all, before you definitely decided to go back to her) — or was she trying to show you how liberated she really was? How much she'd changed? Neither of us had changed, of course, as we were to find out later. And what did you tell her? That you "owed it to Rachel" to go on the trip we'd planned? That it "wouldn't be fair" to "let her down." Something like that, I'll bet. How you used each of us to get your own way. How "liberated" you insisted on us being, when you are the most jealous and possessive man I have ever met. And how we *fell* for it, how we let you give us detentions or gold stars. We had only ourselves to blame. Tomorrow morning, the priest's mother will ring the bells. No *wonder* they make such a brazen sound, no wonder they sound like hooves! And the black widows will begin to assemble and move through the narrow streets towards the church and their flickering, incensed consolation. DA DA DAH DAH DA DAH DA DA DA DA DA DA DAH.

Go look at the snake goddess in the Herakleion Museum. Go think about the Pythoness or Athena — all the great

48

female powers. In the beginning Europe had no gods, only goddesses. Lo, how the mighty have fallen!

One of the things I hate here in this village is all the starving cats. They move quickly and fiercely underneath the tables of the tavernas. Fights break out; somebody gives them a kick. What happens to them in the winter, when there is no one here but the villagers and the occasional tourist? Yannis says that the cats are shot in the wintertime, but I don't believe it. Some of these cats are old and very torn up. Where do they go when the waves crash onto the square and the metal tables have been taken in? How do they survive? Does Dog-Girl feed them *all*? They never come up this street, but remain down on the square. The people here, quite rightly, don't like animals who do not work for their living. They kick cats — even the children do this — and they stone dogs, but they take very good care of their donkeys. I think it is lovely, by the way, that Markos and Heleni have a donkey and two goats, no car or truck, but a television set!

Teneriffe, Las Palmas, Barcelona, Genoa, Naples, Latakia, Limassol, Piraeus. All we had to do, in the early spring, was recite that litany to each other to bring on a severe case of excitement. We had bought books on freighter travel, on how to travel without being rich, on buying a used Volkswagen in Europe and bringing it home. On the wall of our bedroom, we pinned up *National Geographic* maps of Europe, the lands of the Eastern Mediterranean, Greece and the Aegean. We imagined ourselves licking the salt off one another after a leisurely swim in an aquamarine sea. We imagined cheap food and cheap accommodation and all the time in the world to write. We began taking Greek lessons at night school. It wasn't a very good class. Most of the other students were wives or girlfriends of Greek guys and the instructor, who was a marine biologist by profession, didn't know very much about teaching languages. He was always calling for five minute cigarette breaks. You were very quick and I was very

49

slow. You liked that; you liked it when I made mistakes. One of the first things you learned to say was "kake gine," κακή γυνή, "bad woman." I retaliated with "kakos andras," κακός ἄνδρας, "bad man." We are having our ups and downs, our ups and downs, but your novel was going well and things were moving along okay.

Once again you told me that whatever happened to you and me, you knew you would never go back to Hester.

"No," I said, "I doubt if you ever can. You need someone who stands up to you more."

"Well, I certainly got it with you!" But the laughter was friendly and ended in a hug.

"Besides," I said, "mended relationships are probably never very satisfactory. They're like mended crockery. You always have to be extra careful, always."

For our first Christmas, you had given me, among other things: *In Praise of Older Women* and a vibrator. You watched my face as I unwrapped it in front of my daughters; you thought you were being pretty funny (and you were). We had friends over (Robert and his current girlfriend) and we served a big turkey — and I got the feeling that maybe you felt a family wasn't such a bad thing after all. And then we had five quiet days alone while the girls went to visit their father. Virtually all we did was read up on Greece and make love. It was then that we made up our minds that Greece was definitely where we wanted to go. And on a boat, if possible. I come from the last generation who travelled on passenger liners as a matter of course — and I described to you my various Atlantic crossings, the thrill of being utterly "at sea," of being rocked to sleep at night, of sitting in a deck chair reading, of watching porpoises. I had been hoping to go to Europe even before I met you. Now it seemed absolutely the perfect idea. We were both teaching; we were both writing. By taking a freighter, we would have nearly a month off before plunging into work again.

And we would be heading for some place neither of us had ever been before — away from Vancouver and various painful memories. The girls seemed to be looking forward to spending time with their father and I knew how much he missed them. He never left *them*; he left me. This time, he had insisted on having them for two years (as I had just done), not one, and I had agreed. I needed time to be alone with you, to get our rather shaky relationship on firmer ground. I needed to get away, period. Being a single parent is so different from being a "double." I had a lot of guilt towards the children. I am, generally, a very guilty person. I felt they held me responsible for the break-up of our home, because, somehow, I had "failed" their father whom they idealize *and* because I didn't measure up to their ideal. Real mothers weren't supposed to have obsessions like writing or separate identities. It embarrassed them, I think, even when they were proud of me. But I think it embarrassed them because it embarrassed me. And the older two now had a new area in which to accuse me. They had met Hester and liked her (I had had you both to dinner a couple of times). I had "taken you" away from her. The little one was simply and straight-forwardly jealous and she was the one you disliked most.

Sometimes you called her "you little fucking bitch" and *of course*, I defended her. What did you expect?

Once, when I removed the meat without offering seconds you said, "Hold on a minute there, I'd like a second helping."

I explained that I was saving it for tomorrow, that there wouldn't be any second helpings of meat, but there was a good dessert and plenty of bread and cheese in the kitchen if anyone was still hungry.

You said that because you were bigger, you should be able to have second helpings of meat. I said you weren't a farmer who had been out in the field all day, but a writer who'd been sitting on his ass.

Oh well, why go on?

Your cooking day was Saturday because you had never really cooked before and your workload was easier on that day: you wrote, but you didn't have to teach. You never thought about it — geniuses don't think about things like what's for dinner. (Unless they are doing a show-off occasion number or are interested in "the art of cooking.") We either had spaghetti or Shake 'n Bake chicken. "Spaghetti again!" we would say, or "My piece of chicken isn't really done. I can see chicken blood." We were terrible to you, Michael, weren't we? We wanted you to start climbing at the top of the mountain. I could not believe that Hester had always done all the shopping and all the cooking, except for pancakes on Sundays.

"I did other things," you said. I can't remember, but I think "other things" were going to the laundromat and keeping track of the money.

"I never minded doing the washing up," you said.

I laughed nastily, "Anyone over the age of five can do *that* mindless task."

On Sundays, nobody cooked. Hannah did Mondays and Tuesdays; Anne did Wednesdays; I did Thursdays and Fridays; you did Saturdays (in your fashion); Emily set the table because she was only seven. You did not like it that nobody cooked on Sundays, that, if you wanted a "decent meal," you'd have to go out and pay for it. Sometimes we went to the Hong Kong Kitchen on Sunday nights. I paid for the four of us and you paid for only yourself, but still you complained. Sunday had probably been "special" in your childhood, I said, just as it had been in mine. Sunday dinner was the biggest meal of the week. Yes, you said, and you could walk along the streets and smell the Sunday dinners cooking.

"Did Hester cook you that kind of Sunday dinner?"

"Sometimes. But that was different anyway; that wasn't a family."

(It dawned on me then that you had become my oldest child. I was a Mother. Mothers cook Sunday Dinners, ergo. But for once I stood my ground.

"Yep," I said, "it was pretty nice being waited on all the time. But *I* only cook Sunday dinner if I happen to feel like it.")

There might be leftovers in the fridge (from Friday) or there might not. But there was always eggs or cheese or something. Sunday was to be everybody's day off: no cooking and no washing up, except your own.

Sometimes you went out by yourself.

Sometimes you called up Hester and went out.

If I did break down and cook, or cooked just because I felt like it (I'm a good cook — it was principle involved here, not paucity of ideas), the rest of you sat at the table and argued about who would do the washing up, since it was nobody's "official" day. There you were, licking your fingers after spareribs or whatever and arguing over who was going to do the washing up! Sometimes I felt I hated all of you. You *all* wanted me to be somebody I was not, someone I could never be again.

"If you and Michael have a really bad fight, can you kick him out?" Emily asked, looking at me with her big blue innocent eyes.

"Of course not. He lives here. We live together."

"But it's *your* house, yours and Daddy's."

I stared at her, speechless, as the front door slammed.

Hester called you to come over and split up the photo albums. You came back in tears.

Once she suggested that she and I should get together, because she wanted to talk about the problems of a woman living alone. I refused.

In a moment of fury, you cited Frieda Lawrence as an example of a woman who really loved her man. Hadn't she left her children behind and so (in your eyes) proved it?

I tutored Anne and her girlfriend in Machiavelli because the teacher had not really explained him properly.

One of my students called at two a.m. and said that she felt like committing suicide.

"I understand," I said, "I really do."

(But there you were at six a.m., coming back from the bathroom with your beautiful cock sticking straight out in front of you and I, with my eyes almost shut, pretending to be asleep.)

The sea was very calm. There was a hurricane forty miles north of us and you were hoping for a storm. We took turns working in the cabin. I had a morning, then you had an afternoon, then you had the following morning, and so on. The other one went on deck and read, or wrote up notes, or just soaked up the sun. Things were very good between us those nine days and, of course, there were no letters from Hester. They began to arrive when we reached Barcelona. There were nine other passengers, all at least twenty years older than you and they didn't like us very much. We didn't play bridge; we didn't complain about the service; we didn't start drinking at noon. They particularly didn't like you. You were too young, too full of energy and good looks, too sure of yourself. We got stoned at night and mimicked them.

"My wife wants to see ruins. I tell her we don't have to go on a goddamn freighter trip to see ruins. We can just drive through Watts."

One couple had gone down to Mexico in their Buick, but they didn't like it. The wife confessed that she liked being "in the majority." She had one of those girlish American voices and looked like Mrs. Nixon.

We began telling each other our dreams and writing them down. One morning, you suggested that this wasn't such a good idea, telling dreams, so I knew you'd had a dream about Hester. Just after you refused to tell me your dream, you wanted me to come over to your bunk and make love.

"Rachel," you said in Norwegian, "show me your cunt." You pulled the sheet tight over you so that I could see your cock sticking up.

Later, I asked you never to make love to me if you were really desiring Hester. You were playing with my hair.

"I couldn't do that, Rachel," you said.

("I made love to Hester this morning, but I was thinking of you.")

I read your dream, Michael, that afternoon when you were up on deck. You had been fondling a girl's bare breasts, trying to get her to agree to fuck, when suddenly Hester was there on the bed as well, with only her sweater and her panties on. You were shocked because you thought she had gone home long ago. But even after recognizing the other woman on the bed as Hester, you kept on fondling the first one's breasts. So your erection was for the Dream Girl and not for either of us. I laughed and laughed and then closed the book (I knew all the rest of the dreams) and put it back in your drawer.

"Memory is like a long, broken night." Graham Greene, one of my mentors. (But isn't Mentor really Athena in disguise? I can't remember.)

I can hear Markos talking outside, just below, but not Heleni. I know where she is, however. The sound of her loom comes up to me in the still evening. She wanted me to see it the other day. It takes up nearly a whole room in the shed just down the street. There, she weaves the red and black rugs she sells on consignment to a shop in Réthimnon. She sat down at her loom to show me how it worked and, as she picked up the shuttle, such a look of peace and contentment came over her face that she seemed transformed. Weaving is obviously her great joy and perhaps her great escape from the grocery store, the olive groves, the constant domestic pressure. It is a sound I had heard behind shutters everywhere in this village, but I had never seen one of the big looms up close until this week. Now I fancy that sound as the sound of the Cosmic Treadle, the sound of the history of Crete, the sound of Woman as Guardian of Culture. One uses one's whole body at these large looms. Did chaste Penelope weave her tapestry at such a loom?

The women on this street are never idle. They sit on their straight-backed chairs in front of the white houses, spinning or embroidering or winding enormous skeins of wool around their hands. And talking talking talking. The history of the street, too, is being spun, embroidered, wound by these same women. They accept me because I am a "mother" and the arrival of my daughters has become a great event. They see me coming up the street from my swim and they call to me — "Ray-chel," "Ray-chel" (an easy name for them because the "ch" is such a familiar sound) — and run to get me a chair. Heleni's mother laughs as I try her drop spindle. (How easy she makes that look!); the dark-eyed children giggle behind their hands. All the houses are joined to one another, just as all the lives appear to be joined. There are no secrets. Each woman's joy and sorrow belongs to all the rest. It will die out, I suppose, as the life of the square moves up and takes over the village and the luxury hotels continue to be built. One only has to live in Athens for a while to see what will happen eventually. But right now, on Odos Anonymous, a collective life, a collective consciousness, still exists. Was it Plato or Aristotle who said that a village should be no larger than one in which everybody knows everybody else by name? The other day, I witnessed two instances of this. Do you remember the old lady, very old, who keeps the brown hens and rabbits and lives next door to the post office? I was in there buying stamps when the phone rang. The postmaster answered it, listened intently, shouted something in Greek to the voice at the other end ("Hold on," I suppose), and went running out to knock on the old lady's door. He knocked and knocked. No answer. The baker's wife popped her head out of the bakery across the street, asked what was the matter and then, obviously giving him instructions, she popped back inside and he ran off down the street. In no time at all, he was back with the old lady, led her gently to the phone where she listened to whoever it was (an absent son, a daughter) with tears rolling down her cheeks. I was so moved. I left without getting my stamps. I felt I was intruding on something very private.

The second incident involved the town drunk, whom I know you will remember. You used to get mad when I said he looked like a miniature and tacky version of you, but he really does. Same dark curly hair and black beard; same eagle's nose. The eyes are not so fine; Poseidon gone to seed, for Markos told me he was a fisherman once. Anyway, I was in "our" grocery store buying feta and he wandered in, very drunk, and making outlandish requests. (Two kilos of olives, five bottles of retsina, things like that.) There were quite a lot of customers, mostly foreign, in the shop. The woman refused his requests and laughed at him, but gently. She called him by his name, letting him keep his dignity. Eventually, one of the fellows sitting outside at the καφενέon came and got him and led him away, again gently. The woman laughed good-naturedly and went back to weighing out my cheese.

How far we have come from all that, we are so uprooted now, so terribly alone. Think, even of the way we dance — as metaphor, I mean. All last winter, I went to the Aliki Theatre on Thursday nights to see the traditional dancing. So much of it involves a group, involves touching, arms around shoulders, lines weaving in and out. Oh, solo pieces too, but then the soloist usually falls back into the group. The dances are ritualistic, traditional (the women of Thessaloniki still wear the headdress which was given them by Alexander), and beautiful.

Tonight at Zorba's Bar, the tourists will dance to Yannis'

tapes of popular Western music. "I CAN'T GET *NO* SATIS-FAC-SHUN." Everybody will do his or her "own thing." There will be very little touching. Maybe, after midnight, Yannis will be prevailed upon to come out and dance with two of his friends and he will do this, but in a self-deprecatory manner. Although he dances very well, he prefers the pop stuff. He wears cut-off jeans and says "fuck" a lot and both despises and needs the tourists. He has a speedboat and takes people waterskiing, shows off, cutting the motor at the last possible minute when it appears that the boat will fly right into one of the groups sitting drinking and sunning themselves at the little metal tables. In the winters, when the season is ended, he goes to Germany and lives it up. Germany or America (or even England) is his great dream. Or so he says. I tell him there are thousands of Greeks in Montréal and lots in Vancouver. Why doesn't he just pack up his old mother and go? He says she wouldn't like it there and, no doubt, he is right, but also, here, he is in control; this is *his* country. There are probably already twenty "Zorba's Bars" in Montréal.

He was seduced by a Dutch woman when he was seventeen. Now she is back with her very pretty teenage daughter, whom he is very busy trying to seduce. She parades around with a cigarette lighter tucked into her bikini bottoms, while the English girl sits at a table and glares at her over her book. I feel there is going to be a BIG FIGHT soon. Dog-Girl sits at a far table, a flower in her hair, over by the giant chess set, with three or four of the younger fishermen. Most of the time I sit alone, but not always. Sometimes I dance. I still feel I'm convalescing from you, Michael, body and soul, and do not wish to be involved with anyone. The English girl, Fiona, who sometimes comes and sits with me, says Yannis has an enormous cock. But somehow, I am not interested in finding out. Just to be here is enough — I do not (for the present anyway) need a man inside me to prove that I am "real." I'm sure you find that hard to believe. What's the longest you have been without sex since you met Hester? The two weeks after I left you? And then, what did you say in Athens, pointing to yourself? "My poor fucking hand certainly got abused these last two weeks." We had just made love and you were hungry; you wanted to go out to breakfast at the American Restaurant. You wanted to get the show on the road.

Sometimes when I was sitting opposite you, in my bunk, writing away furiously in my dream book, I was simply writing my name over and over again, or "Fuck you, Michael." I would smile and nod and pause and then begin again and then shut the book and put a rubber band around it. Often I hadn't had a dream at all or not one I could remember. I just wanted to annoy you, the way you annoyed me. Putting the light on in the middle of the night to scribble down some dream you had had about Hester. You told Björn, the steward, your poker buddy, that you had a wife down in Africa. Why did you do that, Michael? To "be fair to Hester?" Sometimes I thought, "Well, when we reach Piraeus, I've really got to find the courage to say goodbye to him." But I couldn't. I wanted to be with you for as long as you wanted me. I really began to understand about gun molls and women like that. Women who would take abuse and still come back for more.

You were a bit seasick and I brought you a roll and some cheese and fruit.

"Wasn't there any butter?" you said, looking over the plate. Not "Thank you," but "Wasn't there any butter?"

The artist almost always lives in a Double Now. Therefore, it is not difficult for me to be up here on the roof, thinking of you, and still very much aware of the sound of Heleni's loom two doors down, and the noise of a motorbike coming down that last spiral before the village proper, and the moon slowly surfacing behind the hill. The Beautiful People are finishing their squid or fish kebabs or souvlaki and are thinking it's time to move over to Zorba's and drink a while and observe The Scene. A minute ago, I went down the steps from the roof into my "flat" and came back up with a plate of cheese and melba toast and olives and the pile of all the letters you have written to me. It seems time to re-read them just once more and then get rid of them. Perhaps shred them up and put them in my basket and walk to the end of the pier in the moonlight (I am nothing, if not symbolic) and consign them to the sea. The first ones are not signed — if confronted, would you then have denied that they were yours? Hester is long asleep — you are on your fourth cup of coffee and severely troubled. "We must never never see each other again." Or you are in San Francisco in a small hotel, Hester has gone downtown to cash a traveller's cheque, "You miss me, you don't know what to do." One is just a tiny scrap of paper you shoved into my hand the night you both came down to show me your new second-hand car and we went on to the movies. "Now that I've found you," it says, "I'm so afraid of losing you." Some are from here, to me in Athens; most are from Tanzania. (Even the typed one is here. A brilliant stroke — you knew I'd know it was something awful even before I opened it, for you always, *always*, hand-wrote your letters to me, knowing I preferred that.)

DO NOT COME TO DAR
IF YOU EVER LOVED ME DO NOT COME
TO DAR
IF YOU LOVED ME NOW, OR IF YOU
LOVE ME STILL, DO NOT COME TO DAR.

How silly it all seems now! The mail used to come about one-thirty, shoved through the door of the main entrance of the house where I lived in Athens. I could see the mailman from my tall window where I sat at my blue desk, writing. I waited a few minutes, my heart pounding, and then went out my entrance and over to the one next door and unlocked it. The letters lay scattered on the floor in the hall. If there was one from you, I would take it back to my room and pour a glass of ouzo and read it once, twice, over and over again. They were long letters, full of talks about books and Africa and Canadian Nationalism — brilliant letters really. But always some personal stuff too, about how you missed me, a few freighter memories thrown in, or a scene from Aghia Sophia — you and me at the far beach on Sunday afternoons, rent day and you and Markos getting drunk on Cretan brandy, the Plaka, the Acropolis; what times we had. When I came down to Dar, we'd have good times too. But no sex. Not anymore. Sex was out of the question. I was welcome to stay in the new, larger flat (you would even give up your study) for a week or so at least, and you would have a chance to read my first draft and I would have a chance to read your final one and the three of us would have some good times together.

I was, presumably, to forget that you ever had a body that was close to mine. I was to simply relate to your wonderful head which would float across the table from me in the hot African night at some bar or hotel or whatever, and after all the good food and good chat, the three of us would go back to this large flat and you and Hester would go to bed in the bedroom and I would easily fall asleep in the study. I wouldn't be able to hear anything. You slept with the air conditioner on. You had mentioned that too, in one of the letters.

I refused to come under those conditions.

The fight — the final, "final fight" began.

One of the Southern Ladies on the boat was a charismatic Christian. It had changed her life. Now, when something bad happens, she just puts the burden onto Christ.

"Last summah, ah burnt mah hand," she said at lunch. "Ah spilled an en-tire pan of watah ovah it. The pain was somethin' terrible. Then, ah remembered Jesus."

"And?"

"And ah just stood they-ah with mah hand outstretched and yelled, 'Take it, Jesus, take it. Take this pain.' And you know, He did. He did just that and in no time at all the pain was gone."

I have made up a phrase for the intense glare of the sun against the white walls of the houses in mid-afternoon: "lightwashed." One can hardly bear to look. Sometimes the whole street looks as though it is covered in Royal Icing. It is very hard, with tools as worn as words, to capture the way the street looks in early morning, mid-afternoon, beneath the moon. It is like trying to write legibly with worn-down pencils. I have always longed to be a painter, but never so much since I've come to Greece. The black figures of the two widowed sisters against their white stone wall.

60

The eyes of the children, dark, liquid; the exotic fruit; the fishmonger with his white knitted cumberbund and a scarlet hibiscus flower behind his ear; the light, the light, the light. It is like living in a diamond. Everything they say about the Greek light is absolutely true. I want a palette, not a pen. I have to say that such and such is "like" something else — I have to take the long way around when what I *really* want to do is dip my brush directly into the ocean, the sky, the sun, the eye of Heleni's donkey, the dark beard of the priest, and transfer it all to canvas. I want to *grind up* the white houses and put them there too and *grind up* the baskets of shining eels and capture the precise shade of the bread as it comes out of the oven in the baker's shovel. It is like, it is like — *what* precisely is it like? I pace my study in frustration. I throw myself on the bed and stare blindly at my pink walls.

If I tell you again that the sound of the quail at night makes me nervous, will you remember that it is the ghosts of the German sentries signalling to one another? Can I tell you that the huge tamarisk tree by Yannis' bar seemed to me the other day to be made of soft, green pubic hair? A goat had come along and was standing on its hind-legs nibbling at a lower branch, much to the amusement of the loungers. I was thinking about goats and Pan and magic when lo, the tree, which I had never really looked at before, seemed to be made of soft, green pubic hair.

But you had been here. You could say, "Yes, that's it precisely," or "No, that's not quite it," because you too have seen the tree or heard the quail. You have seen Yannis' face. If I say to you, about his birthmark — "It looks as though someone has flung a glass of red wine in his face" — what would you think? But it is not for you I must write. It is for those who *haven't* been. The artist as transporter? The artist as magic carpet? Both Greene and Maugham did that sort of thing so well, capturing the essence of a place, its "perfume." And *that* done, the next great task — to get the people moving. What are the labours of Heracles to those of the artist, Michael?

You had no phone and began to phone me from pay phones. Particularly, I remember, the one outside the Safeway on Tenth Avenue. Hester was inside buying the Weekend Specials. You had to shout because of all the traffic. We must meet, if only to talk about what to do. Yes, I said, yes yes yes.

She's young, I thought to myself. They have no children. Marriages don't last forever, I know that now. He loves me; I love him. What's WRONG about it? What will I be doing that's so *wrong*?

Before you went on your holiday to San Francisco, we spent an afternoon together in Queen Elizabeth Park. I told you that if we still felt the same about each other in a year, then I would go away with you.

"Will you be my lady?" you asked with tears in your eyes. I nodded. "Yes." I was so flustered, I dropped my camera and cracked it.

Your "lady!" Why didn't I run the other way? Well, I know why. When you are thirty-eight and have three kids and your waistline has disappeared — even if your skin is fine and legs and breasts are good — and some handsome young man comes along and falls in love with you *that* way, that "lady" way! My God, what mortal woman could resist?

We used to take baths together, that was fun. I would massage your cock with my toes. You *liked* my body, you liked it! Once you said, as I was getting out of the tub, that some people might call me plump, but that I reminded you of a painting by Reubens. You made me beautiful. Friends stopped me in the street. "What's happening to you, Rachel, you're glowing!" That has not gone. You gave me back my confidence in myself as a sexual being, that was perhaps the greatest gift you gave. I don't think it will go now; I think it is here for keeps. But in other ways, you were not so generous; in other ways, you were not generous at all. In one of your letters, you suggest that I can *never* live with another writer unless he is "superior" to me (you mean "better-known"). You suggest people of the calibre of Mordecai Richler or Leonard Cohen. Or someone in another field. I am hardly "known" at all. I fear being "known" that way. Yet you could not stand even my little seedling of success, it drove you wild.

Graves says Poseidon was equal in dignity to Zeus, but not in power. "And of a surly, quarrelsome nature." Well, that's you, Michael. After a while, everything I did made you paranoid. In bed one night, I told you something I liked.

"Are you criticizing my technique?"

Do you remember the first time I made love to you? Later, I suspected that it might have been the first time that a woman had actually ever made love to you. You said afterwards that you weren't sure you liked it, that you felt like an object, not a man. I told you that women liked to be the initiators too, like to actively show their feelings. After a while, you couldn't get enough of it, you loved my head between your legs, you loved me riding you.

"I love that," you would whisper.

"I love it because it's *you*."

I miss that, Michael; I miss all our tumbles and romps. Are you different with Hester now, I wonder? She told me once that she is a very loving woman. I do not think she was talking about sex. I suspect she is very passionate underneath, but is so used to *you* making love to *her* that it would not occur to her to turn it around. It is such an intimate thing somehow, it involves such trust on the part of the man. I was surprised, given that you thought I was such a bitch, that you trusted me that way. I could have bitten it off and ruined you forever, couldn't I? (The New Delilah.)

Some mornings back home, you would get up early and go and pee. You always wore old T-shirts to bed, ones that had shrunk and only came down to your belly button, if that far. I would sense your absence from the bed and open my eyes, just to slits, and watch you come back in with an enormous erection. I pretended that I was asleep, but when you slid back into bed, I made a little sleepy sound and turned to you. I loved that — making love in the very early mornings; rising with the sun, my eyes shut.

But in Aghia Sophia, we slept in separate beds with my night table in between. There were New Rules. I was not to turn to you. You were to dictate when and how often we made love. I hated the new (unwritten) rules. I felt you went and did some kind of penance to Hester every time you slept with me. We had coffee every weekday morning at five-thirty a.m. and perhaps a "little chat." No fucking. Nothing to sap your energy. Coffee and a couple of cookies and then off to our respective studies until just before nine, when you put the eggs on to boil and I ran down to the baker's to get fresh bread. Sometimes the bread was so hot I had to carry it back tucked into my shirt because I couldn't hold it. We ate at the little table in our bedroom: soft boiled eggs and fresh bread and "marmelata." Real coffee, not that Turkish stuff which had been a present from the steward on the ship. We talked; I tried not to look at the calendar. You did the breakfasts and lunches; I did the dinners. On Friday nights, you made spaghetti and on Saturdays, we ate out on the street of the tavernas. Weeknights, we were in bed (separately reading and then separately asleep) very early. This was called discipline, this was called dedication.

In the late afternoons, we went swimming and then drank a small bottle of ouzo at one of the nearly-deserted cafés.

"He's very attractive," I said about Yannis, "even with that birthmark."

You were surprised; you didn't think so. We usually sat outside at one of the other tavernas on the square and knew, when the bus from Réthimnon stopped by the little fountain, that the mail was in. We gave it a few more minutes, maybe fifteen, for sorting. (The mailbags were simply flung off the bus by the door of the post office, plop.)

I longed for letters from my children — I had never been so far away, for so long, before. You longed for letters from Hester. Each was jealous of the other, depending on who got letters. Actually, if you got a letter from Hester, you really didn't give a damn how many letters I got.

Sometimes you would come out of your study — when I am sure you had been daydreaming about her or writing her erotic letters — and come down the passage to the minute kitchen where I was wrestling with dinner on the two-burner gas cooker. I wanted to eat out. You (reasonably) pointed out that you couldn't afford it. That you had to save what little money you had left for the trip to Africa.

"Well, you cook the dinners then; I'll do the breakfasts and lunches."

"I don't know enough things to cook."

"Just make feta omelettes and salad, I don't care."

"You know I have to have more than that, Rachel. I can't live on that." (Another missed opportunity to kick you out. Meat was tough and expensive. One night, I said that I was convinced that what we were gnawing at was goat. You couldn't finish your supper.)

You would read me out bits of Hester's letters. Descriptions of her fellow-teachers who sounded awful and to whom she could not relate, descriptions of the heat, the rundown city, the class in African literature she was taking. She was lonely and the school was terrible. I turned the gas down under the rice.

"That's too bad."

"You don't sound very sympathetic."

"She went there as a free agent; you'll be down to rescue her soon. Why should I be sympathetic?"

We ate in stony silence. At some point, I agreed that we should invite her to come to Greece for Christmas. We would discuss the idea of a ménage à trois. "Shelley couldn't make it work," I said. "Or Augustus John." She would go back the first week of January; you would stay on in Aghia Sophia a little longer than planned, until your book was well and truly done and mine was over the hump. Every sensible nerve in my body said this was madness, yet I agreed. I recognized her loneliness (she was writing to me, too) and I did not want you to go. My book was difficult — I was having trouble. I felt vulnerable and helpless and you knew it. No doubt, you wrote to Hester that you "owed it to Rachel" to stay.

You sat down on the edge of the bed. "If I were to write a novel about this," you said, "I would begin with the sentence, 'This is a tragedy about a man who loved two women.'"

You and Hester still shared the second-hand blue Volkswagen you had bought just before the break-up. You said that neither could afford to buy the other out, but I think, from Hester's point of view at least, it ensured a weekly meeting. Often the two of you would go for a little drive or to the Dairy Queen or out for coffee. I tried not to care; I knew perfectly well how difficult it was for her. You would come home with bits of news. Her painting was coming on well; she was going out with a fellow from the Physics Department; she was beginning to love being alone; she had re-discovered her childhood sense of joy in solitude.

Brave words, but I didn't believe them. What else can one say — it's a matter of pride. I could have taught her a few more phrases.

One night, you came home and wept in my arms, terrible, huge, racking sobs.

"What is it? What is it?" I was frightened.

"She asked me if I was happy."

My heart seemed to stop.

"What did you say?"

"I told her happiness wasn't the point."

"Hush," I whispered, holding you tight. "Hush. It's going to be all right."

(The "point" was to be personal growth, the expansion of the soul of the artist. You were a great fan of Stephen Daedalus. You loved me because of who I was, you said. You loved me for my "life experience." You loved me mind and body. Yet I could never offer you the happiness that Hester could, that was clear to you very early on. I didn't *need* you the way you felt she needed you. What you really meant was that you needed her, *you* needed her. Are you "happy" now, Michael, down there in the City of Peace? Has she forgiven you everything by now? Have you wept in her arms and has she rocked you saying, "Hush now, hush, it's going to be all right?")

The tomatoes are ripe now and down on the square I often have a lunch of stuffed tomatoes or stuffed zucchini and beer. The little boats, all strung together, dance in the harbour like clothes on a line. This is such a pretty place. Even the pathetic little fountain, which is more like the brass end of garden hose sticking up in a bowl than anything else, is pretty now with its border of hibiscus. The sea is so many different colours; I am making a list of all the colours it is, and at what time of day. I cannot believe there is no word for blue.

Sometimes, if I walk down to the square early in the morning, before beginning work, the fishermen are pounding octopuses to make them tender. Did you know that they have beaks? Takis, at the bar where we used to sit most often, keeps trying to get me to order some, but I can't. Who said it? "The nightmare spread out on the rock?" The men brought in a huge one the other day, maybe thirty feet long. Wham wham wham, they beat it as though it were washing. Apparently this makes it tender.

That afternoon, I was swimming, not very far out (you know what a coward I am), but not too far from that underwater cave near the cliffs. Suddenly, I was surrounded by what looked like spouts of amethysts, minute jewels gushing up towards the surface. At first, I thought, "How pretty," but then I was sure that it was some huge octopus blowing bubbles. I panicked and thrashed my way out of there quick.

It was only baby jellyfish, Michael. How you would have laughed!

At first, I hated Athens. I missed you terribly and it was, after the first two days, very cold and rainy. Men followed me everywhere, even right to the door of my small hotel. I gave up going out at night and ate at the taverna next door. My novel remained packed in a wicker hamper at the foot of my bed. I knocked on doors in the Plaka, looking for a place to live. I couldn't stop myself from crying. I wrote you letters — "Michael please, I didn't mean it. Michael. Michael." The sound of approaching worry beads made me think of rattlesnakes. Sitting drinking coffee outside the American Express, I wrote brave postcards to my daughters. Views of the Acropolis at sunset.

In one letter you wrote: "It's better this way, you know it, and so do I."

(Hester got your letter, sent you a comforting telegram

and then wrote — you showed me later — "Take care of yourself, for my sake! Rachel can take care of herself.")

"If you come down for a visit," you wrote from Dar, "could we keep our hands off each other? Would we want to try?"

When I was a child, I used to have this curious sense of both participating in events and being outside of them. Perhaps that was my first intimation that I would be an artist? I would be doing something and at the same time watching it as though it were already past. Here, tonight, on this flat roof in this small Cretan village, the feeling is very strong. Perhaps because I know this will all become material; perhaps because I am an outsider here, passing through the lives of the people on this street. I will be, in the end, to them (if they think of me at all), a faded snapshot. The woman who lived over the grocery store one year; the woman with the handsome husband who disappeared (Will they remember me running up the street, weeping?); and soon, the woman with the three lovely daughters. In their great tapestry, I will be just one small stitch. What are you doing right now? What time is it there; I forget the change in time.

The other day, I got a ride to Mires on market day. I wanted to buy a basket, but I also just wanted to walk around. Suddenly, it struck me what a curious shape the plastic baby baths were, rather like coffins, quite different from any baby bath that I had ever seen. And yet, I had seen them before. Where? Not until I came home did I realize they were exactly the same shape as the ancient sarcophagi in the Herakleion Museum. How had this happened? Surely, it was not deliberate? I am still puzzling and delighting over this. We know, back home, how Chianti bottles now come often with plastic "straw" around them. But the connection between the stone coffins and the plastic baths is fantastic.

Do you still have the copy of the photograph of you and

me sitting between the sacred horns of Knossos? Did you see anything at all that day? You were so impatient, so afraid we'd miss the one o'clock bus down to Aghia Sophia. And if we missed that, you would miss the mail. It was my birthday and the trip to Herakleion was a consolation prize for not being able to go to Athens. Hester was coming for Christmas, if she could get all her documents in order. But she wanted a week alone with you in Athens. And you couldn't make two trips; you didn't, as I very well knew, have that kind of money.

Do you know what, Michael? There are days here when I do not write at all. Of course the first draft is done, so I "deserve" a long break. But it isn't just that, or the sea whose warmth and beauty caresses all my senses, or the sun which is drawing the tiredness of Athens out of me. It's the sense of actually wanting to *be* here more, to not feel so rigidly tied to my profession. My essay on Athens moves along slowly, but it will get finished. The revisions to the novel will probably take another year. I do not set the alarm, but wake up when I have finished sleeping. I linger over my lunches in the square. Sometimes I even go out for breakfast. Looking back now, I think that our life here was very dreary, in spite of the swimming, the good talks, the bread fresh from the baker's oven. I understand that obsession, that desire to get something finished and out of the way, but I think we took it to ridiculous extremes. *Always* to spend only an hour for lunch. *Never* to stay too long in the square on Saturday night. (In fact, we only stayed out at Zorba's once.) It wasn't any fun, Michael — there was no spontaneity. Maybe I'm just saying that it wasn't what I really wanted and so I resented what was supposedly joint decisions, but which were really unilateral.

Perhaps I am simply saying that I wanted more hugs and less philosophy. I, who know so well the value of an ordered existence, had one to the nth degree and didn't like it.

And of course there was the ever-present fact that I hadn't "measured up," that I wasn't a "good wife" and would never change, "Kakéh-neck-ka," and that you were leaving me.

Why do women always feel that they are being, or have been, acted upon? I could have got out of the situation at any time. I had some money; I was not afraid to travel in Europe alone; I had a book to write. I could even go home if I wanted to. You were the one who had committed yourself, not me. And yet I felt that you were "doing all these mean things to me," when really you were just seeing how much you could get away with, just putting yourself first, like any normal child. I probably deserved everything I got.

We told Markos and Heleni that your sister was coming to visit us at Christmas.

If I went to the toilet, I could hear you happily typing away in your study, or reciting the latest section out loud. "I'm really looking forward to the three of us sitting here and drinking ouzo and talking," you said one afternoon. The weather was turning chilly and for two days there had been enormous breakers. You loved it; you said you felt as though you were really doing battle with the sea. I was frightened; the waves knocked me over and tossed me towards the rocks. You told me I had to get out beyond that part and I cried because I was afraid and knew that Hester, who was an excellent swimmer, would be right out there cavorting with you. I didn't want to allow *her* any triumphs!

The fishermen began to haul up their boats onto the square.

We arrived in Las Palmas around four-thirty p.m. and were told the ship wouldn't sail until three a.m. the next morning. Neither of us had any mail. We put some necessities in a bag and sallied forth to see the town. We took a taxi with the Professor and Fredericka to a main square and then began walking to the beach, down narrow streets filled with families and sailors (it was Sunday). Lovely golden sand and families, families, families. Bright umbrellas everywhere and ice-cream vendors. We ambled along the promenade up above. Little tables with umbrellas. Lots of cafés. Lots of people strolling up and down. Germans, Swedes, Americans;

some Africans; lots of Spaniards, of course. The whole scene was lively and colourful and after nine days at sea it was lovely to have so much space to walk around in.

We were hailed by two couples sitting on the verandah of the best hotel, waiting for the dining room to open. The men were watching all the beautiful girls in their bikinis. "Bringing your wife to a place like this," said one, winking at you, "is like bringing a ham sandwich to a picnic." He thought this was very funny. It didn't make any sense to me.

We continued our walk. We walked and walked and walked, and then, just as I was about to collapse, you found (as you almost always did) the perfect little restaurant, cheap and cool, where we ate paella and drank a pitcher of wine. Then we went back to the large square where we had started out. By now, it was almost nine p.m. and everybody was there, everybody in town, it seemed, either sitting at little metal tables having drinks or walking up and down in the centre of the square. Just to see the palm trees was exciting and we sat there for almost an hour, sipping Sangria and watching the show. Small children were running about. A baby girl in a long dress and little gold earrings was continually being rescued, just as she was about to disappear in the crowd, by her older sister who couldn't be more than three and a half. The mother was pregnant again. A Catholic country, we said to each other and shook our heads. Secretly, I wished I were pregnant with your child, that I was sitting there next to you, smug and balloon-bellied, for all the world to see.

There were women with dresses down below their knees and teenage girls and boys in "American" clothes — blue jeans and overalls. The sailors looked so young and so clean. Spanish, maybe, or Portuguese. Brilliant white uniforms and little round hats. They moved up and down in groups, carrying kit bags and shopping bags full of souvenirs. The waiters, in white jackets, moved among the crowd, serving drinks and taking orders. It was still hot, maybe eighty degrees, and who wanted to go to sleep? An old whore went by, with pale bluish legs, like uncooked chicken, wearing checkered shorts and high heels, with a faded face. She walked up and down the street a few times and then sat on a bench that encircled a jacaranda tree and flirted with some young men who were teasing her. She became very coy. She swung her purse and rolled her eyes and began to sing. The young men punched each other and began to laugh.

"I love you," I said, touching your hand. (But rather absently, for I was watching the whore.)

At one a.m., we returned in a taxi to the ship. There it was, with a big "H" on the funnel. There was lots of loading and unloading still going on. A strange-looking man in a conical felt hat peered over the side. A couple of other characters eyed me. You, the Protector, said, "Stick close to me." I am glad you are there; I am glad I am not coming back to the ship at one a.m. alone. I remember the old whore in the checkered shorts swinging her purse. This is a culture where a woman would walk out alone at night for only one purpose — at least in the eyes of the men. I went up the gangplank quickly, ahead of you. We were both very tired, but when we got to the cabin, you suggested I crawl into your bed.

At one point, I started to laugh.

"What's so funny?" You were halfway to sleep.

"It wasn't the earth moving, it was the ship." We were underway again.

Michael, surely you did not mind, if, in the square, I said, "I love you" rather absentmindedly? Weren't you making a mental note of the naughty little girl with the gold earrings; the young, dejected sailor who threw himself down at the next table, lost; the gorgeous African woman, her hair a mass of little braids caught up in loops, her dress some long, loose, wine-coloured thing?

Did that make you think of Hester, down there in Tanzania, missing out?

A beer was a "cerveza." "Tropical" was the brand that the young sailor was drinking. Did you make a note of that as well? Did you notice that the whore's legs were bluish white with goose bumps like the legs of an uncooked chicken?

"We have, for all our miseries and self-doubt," a friend wrote to me in Athens, "quite unsinkable egos. And then there's the interest. We walk around weeping, but we're still interested." Yes. And now that the weeping is over (as far as "Me and You" are concerned, at any rate — I've no doubt that I'll fall in love again), I'm amazed at the notes, mental and actual, that *were* being taken. I put my hand over yours and said, "I love you, Michael." I was looking at you and smiling. At the same time, I heard the young dejected sailor order "una cerveza" and noticed that the beer he was given was called "Tropical." His mates came along about ten minutes later, carrying a kit bag loaded with souvenirs between them. They walked away, he scolding them in Spanish.

"Oh, what's the answer for women, Rachel?" my friend wrote. "I still feel we're on the right track — or on some track. You know we can't give up on ourselves, we've got too much invested now!"

Perhaps one of the reasons I get so angry at Hester, and belittle her, is because she has made a choice which I am no longer free to make. She has chosen you over the pursuit of her art. For me, that is no longer a possibility. I want both (love and art), but I can't give up the second for the first. What is that thing by Byron? "Love to a man 'tis but a thing apart. 'Tis woman's whole existence." Something like that. That's what men want to think, that's what they *need* to think, especially men like you — egotists — ambitious and so very insecure. Hester really is the perfect wife for you, so how can I blame you for going back to her? She is the wife as mother (your mother) and because you have chosen to be childless — "at least for the time being" — all her maternal instincts can be directed towards you. She talked one day about how wonderful you were going to be on television, so handsome and articulate. There is absolutely no doubt in her mind that you will succeed, that the fame and recognition you desire will, of *necessity*, be yours.

I remember once, in the seminar, saying how much I was impressed with the quality of the work being handed in. You challenged me: "Well, most of us can hardly be called beginners." I said that anyone in a novel seminar who had yet to complete their first novel was, to my mind, a beginner.

You didn't like that at all. And you particularly didn't like it coming from a woman. Fucking bitch.

Poor Michael! I was the very last person you should have fallen in love with. A published writer; a real mother, in some senses, with real children. Have you ever stopped to think what might have happened if Hester hadn't taken you back? Or did you always know in your heart that she would?

ΠΑΓOΤΑ − "ice-cream." ΦΕΡΡΥ ΜΠΟΤ − "ferry boat." Would you recognize either of those? It becomes a game once one has learned the alphabet. Waiting for the trolley bus in Athens, staring at the sign, I would suddenly realize I was at a "stasis." My notebook turned into two, into three. Still weeping, yes (then), but once again observing. At the Friday street market, a vendor slapped my hands for daring to select my own tomatoes. All the housewives laughed. One of them said to the old man, "Stop acting like a Turk." I wrote you letters nearly every day and missed you, and cried over you often. But I kept a bunch of flowers on my table and studied my Greek and got up at five every morning to work on my novel, amazing myself at my perseverance. Separately, my children wrote wonderful letters, full of news. The months were passing; soon, my daughters would arrive.

You wrote that your book was finished and that with the last of the bottle of ouzo I had given you the night you left, you toasted me. (Hester drank Coke so that you could have the ouzo.) Then you went out and had a fancy meal and *both* of you wished I had been there. I would love to be inside Hester's head and heart and know what she really thinks. Can anyone be that forgiving? It may be true. Or it may just be that she knows what I know in my heart and yet have never learned − that one can catch more flies with honey than with vinegar. You have often said that I drove you back to her and maybe it is so. Each time I criticized her, you felt called upon to defend her; each time I objected to you seeing her, it seemed more important for you to do so. At the time, you said to me, half-joking, "If you love me, why do you hate me so?"

"If you love me, why do you neglect me?"

74

I stripped the bed and left the clean sheets there on top of the mattress. I deliberately "forgot" that the bed had been left unmade. You called me a "fucking bitch" and said you were going to sleep in your study, that I had felt the need to change the sheets and, therefore, it was up to me to make the bed. I told you you were a teenager, that you were a fanatic about order and cleanliness when it was anything that had to do with you exclusively, but an utter slob in every other way. I mentioned the pee around the toilet. I mentioned the fact that you would never dust or sweep our bedroom, but always left it up to me. I mentioned a lot of "facts." I couldn't seem to stop.

You took up your pillow and the spare blanket and I heard the door of your study slam. I made the bed and got in it and wondered what my daughters thought of all that shouting. I wondered why I couldn't just tell you to leave; I felt we had made a terrible mistake and that everyone was suffering because of it. I thought you were the biggest egotist I had ever met; you thought the same of me.

And then you knocked on my door.

You said you came back to get the alarm clock.

I told one of my friends that sometimes you would wake me up at four a.m. and want to make love. Then I could never seem to get back to sleep.

"Rachel," she said. "Do you know how many women wish they had your problem?"

"Needing a wife who would be at home in the sea-depths, he courted Thetis, the Nereid, but when it was prophesied that any son born to Thetis would be greater than his father, he deserted ——."

As we were putting our things away in the cabin, you said that Hester had mentioned "en passant" (one of your favourite phrases, Michael) that perhaps we could all get together at Christmas.

I was holding a pair of underpants. "Where?"

"Oh, I don't know. Maybe she could come up to Greece and we could all go to Alexandria. Then I could go back with her at the New Year."

"I'd have to think about that," I said.

(Hester had written to me before she left. "We both love the same man. Why shouldn't we be friends?")

Did you notice the name of the tug, Michael, which took us out in New Jersey? Did you make a note of it? After the pilot got off and the tug steamed away, there we were, no turning back. Such a strange moment, *that*, especially on a boat, both exhilarating and frightening. There would be nine days ahead of us before we saw land again. The boat didn't sail until seven so the whole scene had become quite magical, as the lights of Manhattan retreated in the distance. My legs were so sore from walking around New York, I had to stand on first one foot, then the other, like a crane. We watched the Statue of Liberty, which was brilliantly lit up, until all we could see was the tip of her torch. There, some trees got in the way. She was gone. Goodbye, America, goodbye, goodbye.

We went below.

I wrote letters up on deck. It was very hot. The day before, we sat still for three hours while a water pump was being repaired. God, it was hot. I could smell fresh bread baking. You came up just before lunch. "What a life!" we said, "and what a *civilized* way to get to Europe."

Markos and Heleni's son was a sailor. He jumped ship in Montréal and finally managed to get immigrant status. Now he sends photos of his pretty wife and their two children. Heleni jokes: "You will take me with you to Montréal." I get a map and take it down to her to explain that I live on the other side of the continent. I do not think she understands how big Canada really is. I'm not sure I really understand. After all, if we push aside the dishes, the map, "χάρτη," fits onto the kitchen table. I have always had that problem with maps myself. In spite of being told the scale, I cannot conceptualize the size. I show her Montréal. There is a little votive lamp under a saint's picture on the wall. The neighbourhood babies lie on the bed again. She makes things pretty, even in that tiny house. You said to me, Michael, that first day, when I spread a shawl upon my bed: "Oh Rachel, you are such a *girl*!" Heleni is a "girl" as well.

In spite of all our doubts last fall, Heleni's flower garden blooms in the dry earth across the road. It is not useful, like the donkeys, like the goats, like the loom, but it is beautiful. It is probably the most useless, maybe the only useless thing she does. I am very moved when she brings me flowers from it.

"We are sisters," she says, and shyly kisses me.

(And all the houses along the street are joined — and all the people are joined as well. And I too, briefly, am joined. I feel nothing could ever, would ever, be *allowed* to happen to me here.)

The watermelon man comes along with his truck full of watermelons; that awful canned music that the travelling vendors use precedes him. I come out of my study and down into the street to haggle with him, along with other women. We surround him and begin to ridicule his watermelons; they are very small; they are hard; they are too soft. Certain sexual innuendoes are made. He whips out his sharp Cretan knife and cuts us each a slice. The watermelon is delicious, but we make faces. Emboldened by the crowd, the fat woman across the street grabs a huge watermelon, raises it above her head and throws it onto the road. It breaks open with a thick "plop." We scream with laughter, the juice from our samples running down our chins. The man looks as though he is about to cry. He tells us we are bad, bad women. But then we all buy melons and he accepts the offer of a hard-backed chair and a soft-drink and soon becomes cheerful again. Street theatre at its best. The Furies Domesticated.

In Athens, when my English landlady and her boyfriend fight so much they scare me and I complain, she tells me it means nothing — "We're *Greeks*," she says proudly, as though that explains it. He has ripped the phone right out of the wall and thrown all the sheets out the window.

In that sense, we fitted in, Michael, didn't we? We fitted in all too well.

The women, especially the older women, often turn their chairs towards the house and away from the street as they spin or embroider or pick grit from a basket of rice. They remind me of small children who put their hands over their faces and somehow think you can't see them.

What do they think as they sit sideways on their wooden saddles, riding home along the beach, their baskets full of greens? What do they think of the girls in their bikinis, the boys in their tight little bathing trunks with EVERYTHING SHOWING, as my mother would have said? Do they simply "not see?" How can they relate to what is happening? The sea, which brings their men a livelihood, also brings an increasing number of Europeans. Do they just accept it as more money for the village? Their sons and daughters put on a second floor above the cube that is their house and hang out a sign:

ARKADI   RENT   ROOMS
ENIK · ΔΩM ·
Zimmer   Frei

They continue to ride their donkeys, spin their wool, have meat, if at all, only on Sundays and feast days. The money goes for a television set, perhaps; eventually, for a van. But for nothing that really eases *their* lives.

Yannis is making good money. He "hires" European girls to help him behind the bar. But his widowed mother continues to get up in the early morning to sweep up the broken glass and rubbish. At noon, he stumbles down from their quarters above. He sprawls at one of the metal tables, his head in his hands and she brings him his first coffee of the day.

You came home from leaving the car with Hester — it was her week.

"Hester's got a job teaching in Africa," you said, undressing. "She's invited me to come and visit."

She had also lent you a book called *Open Marriage*.

We went through the Straits of Gibraltar about three a.m. You had been playing poker and came in to wake me up and tell me that we had won $80.00. Then I drifted back to sleep, but only for a few minutes. A light was flashing against the open porthole window. We got up and knelt, naked, on the little sofa beneath the window. There we were in the Straits and there was Africa — or the lights of Africa! We'd been following the coast all afternoon, but were unable to see it. We had sailed past Tangiers and wished we were stopping there. After sunset, beneath a full moon, the lights of fishing boats had been all around us. Tuna perhaps. Or sardines. Fishing in the moonlight.

You and I went to the bow of the ship. There was never anyone about at night, except on the bridge where it was very dark, as they steered by the stars. It looked as if the moon were floating like a jellyfish, bobbing up and down in the clear blue water of the sky. The sea was silver with moonlight. This was to be our last look at the Atlantic for some time. We started singing "Au Clair de la Lune," sitting against the bulkhead in the dark, tremendously excited. That is one thing that unites us, Michael, and will unite us always. About new experiences, we will both always be kids. You are the most unsophisticated man I have ever met and I can't imagine anything changing that. Fame. Fortune. Nothing. In that way, you are, for me, the ideal travelling companion. You are always interested, never bored. You do not even *pretend* to be bored. Later, when we were kneeling naked, side by side, watching the lights of Africa, I shivered a little, even though it was hot, and you put your arm around me. I was terribly aware of the beauty of your skin, the way your fine hand rested on my naked shoulder. I told myself it was stupid to think ahead, that living in the present was enough.

(The next morning, coming back from handing our letters and cards to the steward, you said to me, "How many of *my* ideas did you steal?")

And now you'll be leaving for home in just a few weeks. You have to get back to your roots, you say. Africa has "released" you, you say.

"The trick is to get outside one's own environment. The North American Indians, many of them, knew this. See the young braves riding ponies out into the desert − they can't go home again until they've had a vision."

Well, my dear, you really rode your pony out into "the Other," − me, as well as Greece and Africa. It seems to me that you found it all too scary, too demanding, but I may be doing you an injustice. You do not clearly explain what your particular "vision" has been, but I do agree about getting out of one's own environment from time to time, whether the environment in question is emotional or "real." One doesn't *have* to leave home, of course. And the security of marriage, one's own land, familiar surroundings, has a lot to recommend it to the artist. "A writer always lives in the Tropics," I read in some book or other. Having "settled" certain things, one can get on with the "real business of life" − one's poems, plays, stories, novels − whatever. One's energies go back to where they belong. Now you are safe again. Sometimes I think that's what I want too. A Leonard Woolf or Robert Browning, someone not just to admire, but to *care* for me, tuck a shawl around my legs or deal with the tradesmen. Oh well, those people all had money − the servants probably did all the work that you and I argued about. Wasn't that the great thing on the freighter? The new-made beds, the dinner gong, the smell of fresh bread baking. Björn offered seconds on the steaks; Astrid handed around fresh loganberry pie with cream. When we were finished, we simply pushed back our chairs, threw down our napkins and left the room for a stroll on deck or (you) for a game of shuffleboard with the husbands.

"The food's very mediocre," one said.

80

"It's the worst freighter trip I've ever been on," another said.

We shook our heads in disbelief.

I told you I didn't like the idea of you going down to Africa to visit Hester. You said, "Don't tell me how to run my life."

I took my empty bottles along to the wine merchants. Down three steps and into a cellar full of barrels. He counted my change in German — ein, zwei, drei. "Danke," he said, smiling, "Danke schön."

"EEMEH KANATHEE," I'm Canadian, I said to him, protesting. It made no difference. His idiot daughter sat in the corner, laughing.

In Barcelona, I told you I knew about Toronto. The man at the next table, asleep, looked to me like Picasso. It was eleven in the morning and we were planning our day. A detective agency was advertised on a building across the street. "Informacion Privada." The night before, you had wanted to know how many pages I had written in my letter-journal to Hannah. I said thirteen. You said I had probably written thirteen just to write more than you. I told you I was tired of your fucking accusations and I wished you would drop dead. I even gave you a shove. You gave me a shove back. We were saved from a fist fight only by the dinner gong. "End of Round Twenty-three," I said. Nothing would tempt you to miss your dinner.

But the next day, there was mail and Barcelona waiting and we cheered up. You were reading out a letter from a mutual friend in Canada:

"Here's a p.s., especially for Rachel:

Every cloud has a silver lining
Time heals all wounds
Rome wasn't destroyed in a day."

You wondered what that meant. I said I had written to him before we left, telling him that you were probably going back to Hester. The fight was on again. Yet, even as we fought, I noticed that the man at the next table looked like Picasso and that the beer was called "San Miguel." You wanted to know what right I had to tell a mutual friend about our private business. I asked you why you had told Björn and the Radio Operator and the rest of your poker buddies about the wife you had down in Africa. And then I pulled out my highest card. I told you I knew about Toronto. (I thought how easy Spanish was — "Informacion Privada." One, un, una, two, dos, three, tres. "Dos cervezas por favor. Gracias.")

I was actually telling a lie. I was just guessing about Toronto. I made up a girlfriend who had once seen pictures of you and phoned me from Toronto when she saw you there with someone else.

"You have your spies everywhere," you said.

I told you I had made a xerox of your Toronto letter, a drawing of cock shooting sperm and all. I told you I was going to send it to Hester. I was lying about that too.

"I've got a present for you," you wrote, "I won't say 'little present.' I'll give it to you on the 15th. It looks like this." The whole letter makes you out to be alone and you weren't; you were there with Hester, fucking happily away, renewing your vows.

How did I know, Michael? I just "knew," that's how, and you did not, in the end, deny it. I said my friend had seen you on Ward's Island with your arm around another woman. So don't tell me what to write or not to write, I said, your letters are full of lies. I told you that it was at that point I nearly decided to call it off — our end-of-the-affair honeymoon.

You were curious. "Why didn't you?" you asked.

Because, Michael, suddenly it was all so funny, so very

funny. And, I felt (wrongly) that with that lying letter you had lost all power over me. I suggested that you met Hester in Toronto in the orange Indian shirt she had given you the year before. You and I had met in Montréal when you were wearing the blue shirt I had bought you for the freighter trip. She had been with you in Montréal as well. She had left for Africa the day before I arrived. You met me at the airport in the blue shirt. You were crouched down and hiding so that I didn't see you when I first came out. I had the address you had sent me, but I was still a little apprehensive. I guess you were watching me and laughing. Then, there you were, laughing, and you gathered me into your arms.

Tell me, Michael — one thing I never got around to asking you. Did you change the sheets in that shabby room on Aylmer Street between the departure of Hester and my arrival? When we had closed the door, you put my hand on your crotch.

"Look what you've gone and done to me," you said. "You've got me all stiff and sore."

You called me from the phone booth outside Safeway. Hester was going to visit some friends in Seattle. I was sharing my house with another family and they agreed to keep an eye on the girls for Saturday night and Sunday. Robert, loyal buddy, went over to stay with his girlfriend and dropped off the keys to his apartment on the way. So there we were again, with the fish tanks, only it wasn't raining this time and I had brought wine and sausage and cheese and bread — all the ingredients for a romantic midnight snack. A part of me felt that Hester had not gone to Seattle, that this was some kind of test and that she was going to be back at your apartment lying in bed, her suspicions completely confirmed. I did not know, for sure, what you had promised her, but I was sure you had told her you would not sleep with me again. When you came back and confessed to her that other time, she told you to go and take a shower. It sounds funny, thinking about it now, but I know exactly what she meant. You had brought me back to the apartment with you, as it were. The smell of our lovemaking had to be washed away.

Perhaps this time she hoped you'd get me out of your system?

Robert had changed the sheets. They were green, with big navy-blue circles all over them, and I wondered if he had done this deliberately. They were very "modern" and unromantic. They looked like bullseyes.

In the middle of the night, I woke up, feeling your absence, and you were standing naked at the window, staring out and crying quietly. I could see your shoulders shaking. I turned away from you and pretended to be sleeping.

I kept telling myself that I had a right to be happy too.

When I met you, I had published four books and had a fifth coming out. I lent them to you shyly, hoping for your approval. You thought they were wonderful. We began to talk on those Friday afternoons after the seminar about the difficulties of writing, and its joys. Looking back now, I can see that this was a kind of "courtship" on my part, but it was certainly not consciously sexual. You were married — I practically knew that from the beginning — and it would seem, happily so. I met your wife at a Department party. She was very small and slim, with long brown hair. She was friendly, but rather shy. I didn't think much about her one way or the other, as I had never speculated on what your wife might be like. It wasn't important to our relationship. I never (at that point) thought about you at all, except on Fridays. Your writing impressed me because of its great energy and its comic sense. It has always seemed to me that I lack a sense of humour. (Not of irony, which is a different thing altogether, but of humour.) I take life, and myself, too seriously. Your novel was about yourself eight or nine years earlier and I marvelled at the distance you had been able to achieve. I thought it was very funny, and touching too. You were a great fan of Henry Miller and of Joyce; an interesting combination. We talked and talked until I suddenly realized it was high time for me to get home.

For months, that's all it was. Just talk on rainy Friday afternoons. That's probably where it should have remained.

"When I married Hester," you said later, "I never assumed it was forever."

A man's first love is never his woman, but his work. That is what he has been taught; that is how he defines himself. What is *left over* goes to his wife and family, although even his close friends may come farther up on the scale than they do. When you came into my life, I already had work that I loved, close friends. It drove you crazy. A "wife" was not supposed to be like that. A "wife" was not supposed to have such definition. You saw all my strengths as "weaknesses" — or flaws at least — in your scheme of things. And I, who had been without love for two and a half years, who had found you and was so afraid of losing you (your words, but I will borrow them for it was equally true of me), began to apologize. No wonder my daughters stared at me contemptuously. I kept telling them that they didn't give you a chance. That may have been so — you certainly stirred up our quiet, essentially female life, and they didn't want you there, but I gave you far too many chances in an attempt to compensate for their hostility. You never had to mind them if I went away for a day or two to do a reading. You didn't have to have anything to do with them at all. After all, Hannah was sixteen. And indeed, they cooked for you, if it was their turn; and if it happened to be mine, I always cooked ahead. You did not suffer *domestically* from my brief absences. Yet I would come back and you would weep and say you had been lonely. I couldn't understand it, because for a long time I did not see what the problem really was. Weren't you pleased, I asked, occasionally to be on your own? Even to sleep alone or go out for a drive alone? You and Hester had done everything together, you said, you just weren't used to this. We took the morning off and went and had a picnic on the beach. I was in despair because I could not make you happy. After all, hadn't you cruelly hurt this wonderful woman who had been loyal and supportive to you for over seven years in order to be free to come to me? I felt I had a *duty* to make you happy; look what happiness you had given up! I "knew" I should tell you it didn't matter whether you cooked or cleaned; I knew I should turn down the invitation to read in Edmonton, in Montréal, even though it was part of my income. And what was worse, I knew that the children were beginning to feel the same way. Because I said that we must all help one another domestically, I was somehow violating my "real" role as a mother. They listened to you and they, too, began to grumble about the Friday afternoon cleaning, the cooking and everything. And my students brought extra manuscripts to the house or phoned up for advice! I never put my foot down, I was so afraid of rejection. I just continued to alternate between apology and suppressed fury. The house crackled with tension.

Hester would call up and ask if we were interested in seeing the movie at the Varsity.

"You go," I said, "I have to help Hannah with her French."

I once saw a sculpture at an exhibition in London. It was called "Large Bleeding Martyr." That was me.

"Oh, but he's so *loving*," she said to me in Athens.

"I don't think he's really very loving at all."

She pointed out your great affection for dogs.

"Sure. But they can be put down or put outside if they are getting in the way. And he hasn't had a dog for years."

"We couldn't; we were moving around too much."

"Of course. It's easy to give someone else's dog a hug or a play-wrestle and then confess how fond you are of dogs. He's not interested in anything or anyone who ties him to some kind of responsibility."

("Except you," I added in my head. "Except you. And you came back to him, good, faithful dog-wife, as soon as he whistled. All kicks forgotten. All those cold nights outside." I couldn't say it to her, Michael, because it was just too cynical, but that's what I was thinking.)

The real laugh on you, Michael, would have been if Hester and I had got it on in Athens!

Who was it that said Prince Charming probably chose Cinderella because she was the only one who could do housework?

What you really wanted (I don't think you knew this then, but perhaps you may suspect it now) was an affair. A hopeless, doomed, star-crossed, passionate AFFAIR. Maybe that's all I wanted as well. Tearful farewells. Renunciation. Sacrifice. All those ennobling *Christian* virtues. (Nothing very noble about the Olympians, remember.) We would all have a good cry and then we would all feel better. In one of your more recent letters, you said, "This way, we can love each other forever." Ah yes, from a distance! Affairs have nothing to do with washing up or toilets or making beds. We cannot believe it when we look at Skeat and discover that "passion" and "patient" come from the same source. I do not think, however, that it will be an easy task to elevate me to that level of unreality again — you know too much about me. I do not know what will happen between you and Hester. You are settled again and snug. I'm sure each is still very careful, and the fact of that, and not liking the school or the other teachers — all that draws you together. What will happen when you go back to Canada in July? What will happen if your book is not accepted? You and I both know that many good books go unpublished because they don't happen to be in style. I have no doubt you will continue to write — I can't imagine you not writing — but your dependence on Hester would become even greater than it is already. You would be the "centre of attention" only in *her* eyes, and, for you, that's not enough.

You are thirty years old and tough. Perhaps bitterness would come only if you hadn't published anything by fifty.

Look at Conrad, you will say now; look at Miller; look at *Ulysses*. I agree. For myself, I feel as though I'm only just beginning. It is easier, because I have had things published, so the "outside recognition," however small, is there. But in terms of control, of the knowledge of writing as craft, I am a virtual toddler. No, you won't be discouraged yet – or not for a long time yet, if *ever*. Hester has nothing to fear.

An English guy I met on the beach told me a very funny story. He and his wife are staying in a "Rent Rooms" with cooking privileges, so she trotted off to the butchers, still in her bikini, to get some lamb for dinner. She doesn't speak any Greek, so she acted out her request.

"Baa-baa," she said, "baaa." The butcher looked at her a minute, then very solemnly went and got her a chicken! "Kotópoolon" (that's what it sounds like); the word for chicken actually means "stupid bird." My teacher in Athens told me that Greek men sometimes use it as a derogatory term for women. But I said nothing, just smiled at the Englishman's story.

Later, his young wife told me that they come from a town – I forget the name – where, during the wars with the French, they once hanged a monkey because they thought he was a Frenchman.

I was afraid of the butcher. Maybe it was just the way he sat on his chair outside the shop, sharpening his cleaver. Great carcasses hung in his cold cupboard, but I didn't (then) know what to ask for. I told you that if you wanted meat all the time, you'd have to deal with him. His prices are terrible and I think he is utterly contemptuous of all Europeans. Do you remember that night we ate what we thought was goat? A very strange, strong taste. Now I eat vegetables, cheese, eggs and yoghurt. When I eat on the square, I eat fish. I don't deal with the butcher anymore.

In Athens, Michael, I gave up buying meat altogether, unless I went out to eat. I ate vegetables and made delicious soups and vegetable curries. Curried eggs. Artichokes with yoghurt and lemon juice. In Aghia Sophia, which, I grant you, had very little in the way of fresh vegetables to offer by

October, I seemed to have some kind of failure of inventiveness. I learned very quickly, later, how to make delicious broad beans in tomato and garlic sauce. Those beans were available at the grocery store where we had shopped. I had a Greek cookbook written in English. My anger blinded me. I did not want to cook at all, under those conditions, and so I did it badly and resentfully. I wanted to eat out at the tavernas. I did not want to *think* about food at all. The freighter had spoiled me. You said the stove was right there; you said you had to save every penny you could. I would have sympathized more with this point of view if the money you were saving had anything to do with us or our life together. It did not. It was to ensure that you got down to Africa and had a little aside as well.

In the Poste Restante, there is a pile of love letters for a guy called Karl Reicker. Practically every day another letter comes in. They are decorated with red heart-seals and little kisses. Obviously Karl is not where he is supposed to be. Maybe he will never come here; maybe she will come looking for him. Eventually, the letters will be returned or thrown out. Is there always one who loves more than the other? Is there always the one who kisses and the other who is kissed? When I was not yet yours, you were mad about me. As soon as you knew I loved you, you began to use that power to "control" me.

Has Hester already apologized for being so "possessive and hysterical" about our affair?

I used to watch the mailman come up the street in Athens. I used to pray for a letter from you, even as they became less and less loving, more "rational" and "friendly." I imagine Karl's girlfriend in Geneva, waiting and waiting and never getting any answer. She watches the mailman come up the street, her face half-hidden by the lace curtain. Perhaps he has had an accident. Perhaps he is lying in a foreign hospital, a victim of robbery and mugging. Should she notify the Consul?

Yet she knows. You always do "know," even if it takes a little time to admit it. I was sitting at the kitchen table

89

making a shopping list. The girls and I were about to go downtown. You said something, I can't even remember what. And I "knew."

"Michael," I said, "are you planning to go back to Hester?"

"If I can work something out with her, yes," you said, "but you've known that, haven't you, for a long time now?"

Then you got up and left the room.

We decided someone had come through the village several years before and unloaded gallon after gallon of surplus paint, in two colours only: turquoise blue and a soft blue-green. For this is the colour of the doors, the older shutters, the trim on houses and boats. It lends a particular charm and continuity to the place and as the tints are both colours that the sea itself takes at certain times, the effect in the brilliance of mid-afternoon can be quite magical. And then, there are bright geraniums in white-painted olive oil cans or broken clay pots. And yellow nets piled in the fishing boats. Yesterday, there was an open van filled to the top with crate after crate of perfect red tomatoes. And two old widows, ominous, against a low white wall of painted stones. In this heat, in this light, the whole world dances and, one feels, it could disappear at any moment, like the Magic Boat, like a dream.

Down under the cliffs, by the walk along the sea, a man sits selling wooden flutes. Nothing mythic about it — sheer commercialism. And yet, as one rounds a corner and suddenly hears that sweet, breathy sound, one stops for a minute, expecting perhaps to see a laughing bearded face behind a bush. But we all know, don't we, that the great god Pan is dead?

"We're unique," you whispered in my ear. "Oh, Rachel, we're unique!"

90

One of the Southern Ladies on the ship announced at breakfast that she felt the end of the world was comin'. When I told her that you were better at Greek than I was, she said, "That's nice. It's always better in a marriage for the husband to be smarter than the wife."

"Why?" I say.

"Why? Honey, just because it *is*!"

One night on the ship, I told you that the reason the Widow does not flirt with you is because you might take her up on it.

"I wouldn't!"

"I know that, but she doesn't. Or she does and she doesn't. You might challenge her just out of devilment. She doesn't want an *affair*, she doesn't want *sex* — look at those spotless white clothes. She just wants a flirtation."

"Maybe I should go and knock on her door in the middle of the night."

"Don't. She'd have you kicked off the ship."

"Maybe I should just go and shake my dingus in her fucking face."

"Do that. They'd probably have you taken off by helicopter."

We curled up in the same bunk, imagining her screams.

"Well, anyway, I know what *you* like," you said.

"And I know what you are absolutely nuts about."

Just a few feet above the ocean, you and I played like dolphins, laughing, cavorting, touching and tasting each other.

"I wonder what Astrid thinks of all those spots and stains," you said.

"I doubt if she thinks of them at all."

"She'll know we've done dirty things."

"Go to sleep. You really are a fool."

I loved the sensation of being rocked and held, not just by you, but by our mother the sea. A breeze blew in the open windows and the waves hissed just below. At that moment, I wanted the trip to last forever.

You sighed in your sleep and pulled me closer to you.

Twenty-four hours in the metropolis and I was writing you EXPRESS letters, with red stickers, from the Hotel Cleo. "Dear Michael, take me back. Let's try and work something out."

We jumped ship at Genoa and caught the night train to Rome. An old man with a limp led us out of the train station and through narrow streets to a pensione on the sixth floor of an old building. I was afraid of the cage-like *ascensore* and walked up. By the time I had arrived, you had already seen the room and taken it and Alfredo, cap off, was drinking coffee with the rest of the family in a corner. The room was small, but it had a tiny balcony, and we were in Rome.

"Next time I come," you said as we walked along behind Alfredo, "I'll know this is the district and won't need any help." I tried not to hear. The next time you came, you would be with Hester, not with me.

A double bed was a "letto matrimonio," I read. We didn't ask for one; it was given to us.

We left our bags and had breakfast and went out.

I have so many snapshots of you in Rome, Michael. You in front of the Victor Emmanuel Monument. You kneeling by the Tiber. You sitting on the steps at St. Peter's. You everywhere. You were always wanting me to take your picture in front of something historic or picturesque. Rarely did you offer to take mine.

In the Forum, we had a fight because I asked you to stand against a crumbling arch and you started telling me, as usual, how to use the camera.

"It's only a snapshot," I said, "I'm no photographer."

"I don't want to be in the picture if it's going to turn out badly — and it will." You walked away.

I followed behind you, down a line of broken statues.

Gods? Goddesses? Senators and ladies? I did not know. A single yellow rose bloomed against a damaged marble foot.

We climbed some stairs and I sat down on a bench, utterly overwhelmed with the futility of the relationship and your bad manners. "Love Among the Ruins," but the ruins seemed to be not the grandeur that was Rome, but our life together. It was only the beginning of September. Yesterday, when the agent came on board, you had a letter from Hester. You went into the cabin to read it and locked the door. How was I going to keep this up until the New Year? I had thought I was so "modern." It had become a joke: "We're just having the honeymoon at the end." I sat on a stone bench with footsore old ladies and began to cry. I was afraid of the power you had over me, afraid I might go mad.

Eventually, I wiped my eyes and told myself I'd asked for it and went to find you. I climbed more steps to a small pavilion where people were looking at the view. You weren't there. A park with many paths spread out behind me.

"Michael!" I called, "Michael!"

People looked at me and smiled. You had the maps, all the Italian money, the keys to the pensione, whose name I could not even remember! How casually (because I knew you liked being in charge) had I handed over all responsibility to you. I could not even remember the name of the street the pensione was on. Now I really had something to cry about.

"Michael!" I called, "Michael!" starting down first one path, then another.

We had planned to go on to the Colosseum. I could see it in the distance. Perhaps I should simply go there? Perhaps it would be better to try and find the Embassy — to explain my stupidity and see if they could help me. My passport and traveller's cheques were locked up at the pensione. They had given us a card with a map on it: that card was in *your* wallet. Since the death of my marriage, I had travelled a fair bit on my own. And the whole family had travelled before that. And I, as a student, had even travelled before that. I could speak a smattering of Italian, for God's sake, and had been to Rome before. I was not a middle-aged virgin afraid of being raped or swindled. I must calm down and think of the best thing to do. The pensione existed. Alfredo was probably at the train station right this minute, drumming up business. I would go there. I would ask for him. Perhaps there would be a list of pensiones at the Tourist Office in the station. If I saw the name, I was sure I would remember it. And then, and then? Well, I would go there and get my passport and my traveller's cheques and move somewhere else. I would leave you a note saying that I'd see you back at the ship. I would enjoy the beautiful city on my own. I would go to the Colosseum; I would take myself out to small restaurants in ancient squares and damn the expense. I would have a good time. I would have a break from you!

I stopped calling your name. I started back down the stone steps. I needed to get out of the Forum and begin the long walk to the station. "Dové," where? "Dové the train station?" Stazione? Stazione, that was it. Who cared whether it was masculine or feminine. Dové stazione? Stazione tréno. Masculine probably. Tréno was at least masculine. You, of course, had the phrasebook as well. How we had laughed the night before as we read out some of the Useful Expressions: "What is the matter?" "I don't know." "I don't know anything about it." Quell' uomo mi seque dappertutto. "That man is following me everywhere." It wasn't going to be easy, with no map.

Dové la stazione tréno? And then, to find Alfredo or the name of the pensione. Something about cowboys? Yes? No? I couldn't remember. I was a bit faint from hunger and excitement, but I'd be okay. Walk slowly, stick to the main thoroughfares. Ask directions only of women or families. Why had I not brought any money with me? It would have been nice to take a taxi. I did want to get everything settled before the siesta. Something about cowboys. It was on the tip of my tongue.

At the foot of the steps, I met you coming along the path. "Get over your snit?" you said.

We sat outside a restaurant in the Piazza Santa Maria in Trastevere. It was Sunday, and after making love to the sound of bells, we had walked the city for eight hours. Then, back to the pensione to shower and change before going out again. We ate scampi and drank wine and talked to the waiter who had once been a steward on a freighter.

"What a lovely, lovely city," you said. "I'll always be glad we did this."

Two old men were serenading us with a violin and a guitar. Small boys moved among the tables selling roses. You didn't buy me one, you thought spending money on flowers was silly, but you said you felt like it just the same.

"Coming from an old miser like you, even the thought is nice."

"Do you think I'm a miser?"

"I don't know. You've had to be. I recognize where it comes from."

"Would you really like a rose?"

"Yes, I suppose I would."

I pinned it in my hair.

"We're a couple of romantics," you said. "It will be our downfall."

"Did you notice the colour of the houses?" I said. "Especially in the old section? Ochres and ambers and burnt sienna — all those beautiful earth tones."

"And everywhere you look, an Imperial Eagle or a saint, Caesar or God."

I showed you the stamps I'd bought in the Vatican book-shop.

"Look at them closely."

"?"

"It's a group of women sitting at the feet of Jesus."

"So what?"

"Well, I wish I'd got more of them. They're 1975 and celebrating International Women's Year, for God's sake. 'Hail Mary, Blessed Art Thou Amongst Women.'"

The name of that place was the Pensione Corallo, Michael. Why had I forgotten it — I, who, as you often say, have a memory like a tape recorder? What was I trying to do to myself?

I had to say nasty things about Hester because I did not want to believe in her niceness. *She* kept telling you she wasn't nice — why couldn't you say it too? When she got the job and then invited you down to Africa "to visit," I think she knew exactly what she was doing. She was saying to you, "Look how 'liberated' I am, I'm not asking you to come to me, I'm just offering you Africa and my company and no commitments." She even offered to pay your way. I was furious. I said I thought it was something we should discuss together. You told me not to tell you how to run your life. You told me I was a jealous fucking bitch. You pointed out to me that I had separate friendships. I said yes, but it was hard to keep them up when you didn't even want me to go out to lunch with any of my friends, female *or* male. How would you feel if I casually mentioned that I was going to spend a month in Paris with one of them next year? You said that was different, I'd just be doing that to get at you. It was "different with Hester;" she had been your wife and friend for seven years — it was a different case altogether. All the more reason for me to feel threatened, I said. She wants you back; she makes no secret of it.

She had never at any time for months and months, you said, made any mention of wanting you back. As a matter of fact, she had just mentioned how much she was enjoying her freedom. Waking up alone on Sunday mornings, for instance, then going to Smitty's Pancake House with a girlfriend.

"Notice how she indicates that she's not involved with anyone else."

"Maybe she just has the courtesy not to throw it in my face. She has mentioned someone in the Physics Department once or twice."

"Why doesn't she invite *him* down to Africa?"

"Maybe she has."

"Are you going to sleep with her when you go down?"

"I don't have to answer that."

"No, I guess not. So long as you agree that I can sleep with whomever I want while you're gone. Greeks, Arabs, one-eyed Egyptians, fellows passing through."

"You would, too."

And so on and so on and so on.

My theory, for a long time, was that you fell back in love with Hester because she got a job in Africa, maybe the ultimate Romantic Dream. Now I think Africa was just an excuse. You wanted to go back to her, you missed the security that a woman like Hester gave you and, this way, the two of you could "start over" in a new place, far, far away from me and any threat that I might pose. Gradually, "going down to visit" (I had finally accepted that you would go there for about a month the next year and you talked a lot of big talk about going down the Nile and wrote away to the Egyptian Consulate in Washington, D.C. for information) became "getting back together;" at exactly what point I do not know. You and I were fighting a lot. Emily and I had accepted an invitation to go on a picnic with an old friend, who was also an ex-lover. There would be others present, but you were outraged and threatened to move out. We had talked and I said your going out with Hester threatened me in the same way. You agreed to cool it down, *not* see her off in New York, for example, but wait for me in Montréal. Probably every time I told you how threatened I was, your power became greater. Hester was about to leave for Banff — she invited you to spend the day with her before she left. Of course you went and of course we had a huge fight about it later that evening. Ironically enough, it was Greek Day and we walked among the crowds along Broadway, me crying and you stomping ahead. You went to your study to "write a letter." It was probably then that you actually proposed the new plan. When you went down to Africa from Greece, you would not return. But you didn't just chuck me, oh no. You *also* wanted to go to Greece and you wanted to go on a freighter. "Liberated" Hester ("Wonderful woman," you thought, with tears of gratitude springing to your eyes) said that was fine. I'm just guessing, Michael, but I'll bet that's pretty close to the way things were.

The girls went to spend a month with their father, and then, they were to come back to me for a month before I left. You would go on ahead, to "see your family," to "have a little time to yourself." By now, of course, you had admitted that you and Hester were getting back together. You took out piles of books on East Africa from the library and ignored anything Greek. You went up to the University

Clinic and got extra shots for things like plague and cholera. I hoped you'd have some terrible reaction. I hoped you'd turn back or get huge sores all over you. You mailed most of your possessions home in crates, to your mother in Montréal. I went around crying; you, on the other hand, had never been happier. It had "all worked out for the best."

On Friday afternoons at six o'clock, Hester would call from Banff and you would take the call upstairs, pulling the extension phone into the bathroom and shutting the door. Once, the door swung open a bit (I was sitting on the bottom step, my head in my hands — I'd just come in from shopping and could hear the murmur of your voice upstairs, behind the bathroom door) and I could hear you say, in that soft, loving way you have, "I love you too."

I went to put the groceries away. You didn't come down for a long time. You were in your study, either masturbating or writing Hester a letter. Just as you used to do with me. I began to think I would probably go mad before we ever got to New York City. I also began to wonder about myself, what kind of masochism was driving me to accept such an impossible situation. I felt like the ninety-pound weakling who just sits around and whines about all the sand being kicked in his face. I was very angry, more angry with myself than with the guy who was doing the kicking. I paid a visit to Robert.

"Do you really want to go to Greece with him?"

"Yes. I guess so. I love him."

"That's a woman's word, I don't know what you mean. You tell me he's nasty and mean and selfish and you feel you're being used and yet you 'love' him. Aren't you just afraid of being alone again?"

"Maybe."

"Well, you have to decide the risks; you have to decide how strong you are. I think Michael's been good for you, but if it's over, it's over, just let it go. I think you're pretty strong. Go have a holiday, fuck a lot of Greeks, get Michael out of your system and then get down to your book. You've got a year off — go do what you planned to do all along."

Sound advice. Robert and I had drunk a bottle of wine. I drove home, wine-strengthened, to tell you to move out. No hysterics, they were over. It was true, you'd done a lot for me. You had touched a very deep part of me. Perhaps it had been my last, necessary unfolding. I was lending you the money for the freighter trip and I might have to sacrifice that; I couldn't really see sharing a cabin with anyone else. You had said recently that I had driven you back to Hester. It was probably true. I couldn't deal with you, your jealousy and resentment of the way I lived my life. We were *both* being diminished by our relationship. I got out of the car almost cheerful. There was a note on the kitchen table saying you'd driven to Bellingham to see a friend and would be back very late. I fell asleep, and when you came in, I stirred and you kissed my eyelids and touched my hair, and then you undressed and got carefully into bed. I never said a word.

They *must* have had a name for blue. What did they call that amazing colour they used on their frescoes? Someone has suggested that they didn't "see" blue. Why not? Who said it? Of all colours, why would that be the one they didn't see? Or was it, as I have found, that the sea, "í thálasa," was so many different colours they could never agree on a general descriptive shade which would "cover" them all? But then, I think of the Eskimo and snow. Surely, that which was not just beautiful but so important economically would be very precisely described? It's a mystery to me. If they could create blue pigment, then they could see "blue." Another thing to make a note of and follow up when I get home. And what did the Minoans use to get that "blue" they ground for pigment? Perhaps that's impossible to find out, but it should not be impossible to find out what it's called now. Some of those colours are obviously made from various kinds of earth. But the blue, the nameless blue? From the sky, ὁ οὐρανός? From the sea?

Posto Riservato Agli Invalidi Di Guerra E Nel Lavoro. "This seat reserved for those crippled (or wounded) by war and by work." Do you remember that sign we saw in the buses of Rome and on the train to Naples? For a long time after you left, I felt like one of those "Invalidi." I felt fragile and convalescent. Perhaps you and Hester felt the same? "The Last Showdown," like something out of a Western, and then a couple of weeks of forgiveness.

(Hester was very forgiving and loving now that she absolutely and for sure had you back. She confessed that she had felt all along that the ménage à trois was just one of your fantasies and she had come up to "help you act it out." Get it out of your system — or words to that effect. She said you live a great deal of your life in a fantasy world and that she becomes more and more practical as your fantasy takes over.

"I believed in it," I said, "*I* thought it might work."

"But you're the one who broke it up," she said.)

Then you were off. She, one day; you, a couple of days later, to give you time to say goodbye. You flew to Addis Ababa and then to Dar. We didn't sleep together, the excuse being that I had my period rather badly and you didn't want to make it worse. I said I would like then, to make love to you. You said no, let's wait until we can enjoy each other. I doubt if you had promised Hester (then) never to sleep with me again. You didn't need to; she didn't need to ask it. From the time she arrived, she was really the one in control. We had thought of going to Turkey and were quite excited about it. She said she had had enough of exotic places for a while — Athens was fine with her. She wanted to see something of Greece and so we revised our plans. She was worn out, you said; she was very nervous and worn out. I told you I was worn out too and you said yes, we were all worn out (accusing voice), but Hester had been Alone in Africa, she was the most worn out. Greece was still Europe, after all — the shock was not so great. I said I'm sure that's true, although Athens seemed pretty "Other" to me when I arrived at Piraeus from Crete with my wicker hampers of books and manuscript, my backpack, my address of the only hotel I had heard of that was clean and reasonable.

It was pouring with rain and I had checked my things in the baggage cage because I was travelling as a deck passenger. I had wooden counters for redeeming them. Everyone was shouting and waving their counters; and, as far as I could see, I was the only female in that crowd. I am not as small as Hester (taller and fatter), but I'm not very tall. Men kept pushing and shoving. I wanted the sheer *bulk* of you there to help me. Finally, I said to a prosperous type next to me, who had just given his counters to some lackey who had come on board, "Greek men are very bad," in my hesitant Greek, and smiled a sad smile. He grabbed my counters, shouted for his lackey and I had my baggage in no time. The honour of Greece was at stake. I found a taxi, found the hotel, and went up to my room, where even a distant view of the Acropolis didn't prevent me from bursting into nervous tears. It was eight o'clock in the morning. I saw you sitting at your desk in your study. I wanted to go back. I wanted to tell you that I would agree to anything, anything at all, if only you would stay with me a little longer. Two days before, I had been in such an agony of rage and despair that I could not speak properly or stop shaking. Why in hell did I want to go back? How silly, how contemptible that woman in the Hotel Cleo seems to me now. Without dignity, without pride — the worst kind of emotional parasite, utterly denying the strengths she very well knew she had, wanting to say, "Look, I'm helpless, poor me. You must rescue me." A part of me stood away from this Creature and sneered; this was not love, it was some horrible, perverse negation of will. And for whom? An egotist, a bully, a man who only had the power over me I chose to give him. I *loved* him? Loved?

Athens was out there: present and past. I had been planning a trip to Greece before I ever heard the name Michael O'Brien. Money. A room of my own. My manuscript in a wicker hamper at the bottom of the bed. I tried to remember a line from *The Faerie Queene* about one of the men who was changed into a beast by Circe. It's a famous line, but it escaped. He can't, or won't, change back again.

"Let Grill be Grill." That's all I could remember.

You were not going to change, but I could certainly change back again — into the person I was before I met you.

"And keep his swinish ways." Did that come next?

I would have to find an apartment or rooms. The hotel, which had no monthly rates, would be too expensive in the long run. I would stay a week and pamper myself and eat out but, at the same time, I would look in the papers to see what might be available. Christmas was coming up; I would have to say to myself that it was just another day. I had never been without my children at Christmas.

(And a small voice said, "You don't really have to *prove* anything; you can go home.")

I took a lukewarm shower — a luxury! I washed my face and brushed my hair and went downstairs to enquire where I might get breakfast. The old man behind the counter wore a black beret and spoke excellent French. He said he had learned it in Egypt during the War. I realized how little I actually knew about a war ("The War") which had shaped my childhood. I wasn't awfully interested in contemporary history and knew only that "we" had won, that Hitler and Hirohito and Mussolini had been dreadful men. One of my earliest memories was of huge posters in our town with pictures of those three and the warning, "Shh, the Enemy Might Be Listening." Why had he spoken French in Egypt of all places? What had happened there? The French seemed to have been everywhere. I wanted to find out. He led me along a narrow street to a small bakery/café which was already open and he made sure I knew the way back. Once again, as in Rome, I felt free, adventurous, optimistic, only this time, I wasn't going to back down. "Let Grill be Grill." I had made a move; I had ceased to be "acted upon." I ordered a coffee and a sweet bun and thought, "Athens, I'm in *Athens*!" I decided to finish my breakfast and go see the Acropolis for starters. I would go every day until I knew every inch of it. I would study Greek. I would write the novel I had come to write and take notes on the life around me. I would meet people — interesting people. I would re-read Sophocles, Euripides — everything. You could go back to your wife and go down to Africa to some stupid school. What would you learn in a place like that? I wanted to be amongst THE PEOPLE!! I couldn't wait to pay my bill and get going.

I phoned Robert from the hotel that night. He was very sleepy.

"Rachel, do you know what time it is?"

"I'm in Athens. I've left him."

"Good," he said, "it's high time you got tough." And

then he put the phone back on the hook.

Two days later, harassed, frightened, lonely, I wrote you, begging you to take me back.

Your "octopus-love," another name I have for it. Suffocating, devouring, ruthless. My octopus-need.

I went up to your apartment to ask you about a book in the library. You and Hester were just thinking of going there yourselves — we could all walk over together. As a matter of fact, you knew exactly where that book was, if some fucker from the seminar didn't have it out. Hester went to get some art books and you and I went down into the stacks.

The book was there. I think it was one of Bukowski's books. We would have invented something else if it hadn't been. You reached up and got it and then turned to put your arms around me. You kissed me and groaned. Michael, you *groaned*! Nobody had ever groaned when they kissed me before. And I saw it not just as a groan of passion, but one of despair. My heart turned over.

We staggered up the stairs and went to join your wife. I'm sure she must have known. I felt as though my face was on fire; my whole body was buzzing.

I declined coffee and rushed off into the night. I remember driving down Tenth Avenue in the rain, terribly upset (and yet enthralled by that groan). The house was quiet when I went in. The couple I shared with were in the kitchen drinking tea and eating brownies. All the kids were asleep.

I went upstairs and wrote you a letter: "We must never, *never*, see one another alone again." In your apartment, Hester had gone to bed and you were sitting at the dining room table writing me a similar, more fanciful note. "I'm on my fourth cup of coffee. . . ."

I was out the next day when you cycled down to deliver yours. I was up at the university putting mine in the Grad Student mailbox.

A labyrinth, a maze, may possibly be a dance then, a ritual performed by chosen youths and maidens. No Theseus. No Ariadne. No Minotaur. All those metaphors for something else. What? The Minotaur was "caused" or was a result of Minos' failure to obey the rituals, his trying to get away with something, keep something that belonged to the god, not to him. And so his wife lusted for the very sort of animal he himself had coveted too much. And thus the monstrous child was born and had to be kept hidden.

What does it mean? The bull is everywhere in Minoan art and culture. He is magical and his horns are the moon. How did Passiphae feel when he mounted her — his great cock entering her from behind? Did she enjoy it? You loved me to kneel and turn over. Why? Was it more exciting for you that way? (Do you remember the Hotel Gotham and the mirrors? "You like taking it from behind," you said. But really, it was more that you liked giving it.)

On the road down to Aghia Sophia, in the rented Volkswagen, hungover from the wine and the terrible fight on the ferry boat, we stopped at a tiny village café. We wanted coffee and we wanted "asperini." You had thrown up in the Avis Rent-a-Car bathroom; I had felt like it. But we were friends again, moving — a new adventure ahead of us.

A fine-looking man who turned out to be a major in the army, came in and began speaking to us in English. He treated us to coffee and even rustled up one aspirin. I suggested you take it; you were doing the driving. Some of his cronies shuffled in and the old woman who had been summoned from the back to serve us lit the stove under the little brass coffee maker. The major began to show off, asking us questions in English, repeating his questions and our answers in Greek.

"Do you have any childs?" We looked at one another. "My wife does," you said, "but by another husband." This was greeted with great amusement.

"Boys?"

"Girls."

He shook his head and tsk'd.

"Ah, you must drink plenty of Cretan wine and soon you will have a son named Minos."

Even the old widow cackled with laughter at this.

I would have had your son, Michael — even a son named Minos or a daughter named Ariadne. ("A-dón-ees! Aph-ro-dée-tee!") But you didn't want children, did you? — Do you? Or not yet. And Hester? She didn't want *me* to have a child of yours. It was one of the things which led to the final showdown. She told you she would leave any ménage if I got pregnant. She said she hated herself for feeling this way, but that's the way it was. And you, having promised to keep her "secret" came and told me, quite literally "came" and told, for I was lying in your arms and we'd just made love. You said you would have to leave as well — if that happened. You "owed it to Hester."

Last night, a couple of men were already playing chess on the giant set outside Yannis' bar. Loungers gathered to sit on wicker stools and watch. I wonder where the chess set came from originally? It's terribly chipped and cracked. One of the knights has lost his head; a black bishop is held together with string. This could be wonderful in a movie, start filming from up at the top, come down down down all the steep little streets, the steps, forty-one down to the cement ramp which leads to Yannis' (ZΟΡΜΠΑΣ ΜΠΑΡ) and the enormous chess game under the tree. There is music now, one can hear it — Neil Young singing something a bit dated, maybe "Heart of Gold" — or "Saturday Night." And one can see wet marks on the blue directors' chairs at the metal tables, left by the asses of late swimmers. One of the two chess players — the man in the hat — kicks over the king in a graceful gesture of defeat. Everyone laughs and applauds. He will be the hero of our story.

And what then, what then? A part for Yannis, for Yannis' cranky mother? For Dog-Girl? For the handsome young fisherman over there on the beach who is repairing and repainting his boat, helped by the girl in the white bikini.

Or begin it at one of the big café/tavernas under the awnings. A European couple. She is very young; he is twenty years older, but very handsome (of course). She is bored, bored, bored. Takis, the owner, comes with a fresh paper tablecloth which he clips to the corners of the table with plastic pegs. She sighs and stretched out her pretty brown legs. He returns with a pink plastic basket containing thick slices of fresh bread, two knives, two forks, two paper napkins. She picks up the menu which has been typewritten by someone for whom English is obviously a second language.

"I think I'll have some of the roast lamp," she says, sarcastically.

How about that? A Hemingway beginning.

Or how about Heleni milking her goats or the priest's mother ringing the church bells, or me, sitting on a rooftop above the crooked whitewashed street, Odos Anonymous, drinking retsina, drying my hair? What is that European woman doing there? Who is coming up the steps to the roof to join her?

(One must first get in the noise of the rusty-throated donkeys, the roosters, and the vans with their awful canned bouzouki music.)

Or take you, Michael. It is late November. Most of the fishing boats have been hauled up onto the square. The sea is rough and maned with foam. There is hardly anyone about. A young man of about thirty has just sat down at a nearly-deserted café on the square. The proprietor brings him a small bottle of ouzo and two small glasses. The young man shakes his head sadly. "Ena potiri," he said, "One glass." The proprietor looks at him and shrugs. How about *that*, Michael, how's that for openers? You gave me the idea.

"It's the little things that make me want to cry," you wrote. "Ordering three small loaves, not five, at the baker's each morning; that extra glass for ouzo at the café; shopping at the grocery store down the street, scanning the shelves alone, nobody to turn and cuss at; coming down the mountain to meet — no one. The leap of the heart, looking down the mountain at the benches in the square — Is she there? No, of course she's not. "Oh, love. What a mess."

I got that one at the American Express in Athens.

106

HOTEL ACTEON
HOTEL AGROPOLIS
HOTEL ASTORIA (Lux)

The ones way at the top look pretty fancy. I wonder how much they charge? I give this place two years maybe, before it is utterly ruined. Now the delicate balance between the village people and the intruders is still all right. The postmaster calls to me as I walk in the door that I have some letters. The money-changer in his little store gives me a sesame seed cake after he changes my dollars. Most of the time, everybody seems pretty cheerful. But the tours will come and the huge hotels at the very top will be completed and people will complain about the noise of the donkeys and the roosters, and entrepreneurs from Herakleion and beyond (Athens, America) will convince the people on the small streets like Odos Anonymous to sell out for cash. I went to Aghios Nikolaos, Michael; there are no Greeks there, not really. The British located a TV series there, "The Lotus Eaters." It's just a high-priced watering place now. Lovely for tourists, I guess. The *Blue Guide* says it is "the least Cretan place in Crete." It will happen here on the south coast, too. The sea, which has been the benefactor of these people, will, in the end, destroy them.

I would be downstairs, working at my desk, a small framed snapshot of you in front of me. The girls were all at school. I could vaguely hear the thud of your typewriter keys upstairs, but it didn't really bother me. There we were, two geniuses at work, and tonight, which was my cooking night, I was going to make something special — pot roast with wine, apple cake for dessert. It had been a good week. Things were going to work out. Naturally, it took everybody time to adjust and re-adjust. I shouldn't have worried so much; I probably caused a lot of the tension myself.

I usually stopped for lunch when you did, because my study was next to the kitchen. I was very aware of your presence. That day I said to you, "You know, Michael, I think we're going to make it." You suggested maybe we go upstairs for half an hour before we went back to work. I took the phone off the hook and followed you up.

E Pericoloso Sporgersi
Ne pas Se Pencher au Dehors
Nicht Hinauslehen
That was another sign we saw on the train to Naples. Well, I suppose it is dangerous to "lean out" of any situation. Or to lean out too far. You were probably smart to stick your head back in. You were just lucky that Hester never really got off the train.

Outside the fishmonger's the other day, there were boxes with "Venus" stencilled on them. *Venus.* I'm surprised the whole village didn't disappear with a thunderclap. Oh well, Aphrodite is a Cypriot; perhaps she isn't looked upon with much favour here.

I say to myself sometimes that I wanted something permanent with you, something that would have grown and deepened. But I wasn't willing to change any more than you were. And if you "got off easy" (as I sometimes bitterly think), well, I didn't do so badly either. You made me bloom again, Michael, and you taught me just how strong a woman I really am. I do not *need* to be "looked after" or "defined," even if I might want it. I do not think that my "greatness" (you said it, I didn't) is my "cross" (also your word). In terms of men like you, perhaps, for they will never stay long with women like me. But there are others — where I'm not sure, but they're around and they aren't threatened by a woman who is more than a shadow. For you, it could have been a disaster. Maybe if you'd had one book out already — I don't know. Outside recognition certainly does help with one's inside fears. It was sad that you came to believe that anything nice which happened to me somehow lessened you in the world's eyes.

And Michael, think on this, dear, you have given me so much material!

Every time I see an aquarium from now on, I will think of you.

If I put your groan in a novel, Michael, everyone will laugh. Groans (except of lust) are out of style. I think your dilemma was real — I will always believe that. You did not want to hurt Hester, who had done nothing but good to you; and yet you did not want to lose me.

We went outside into the soft April rain and Hester, her arms full of art books, invited me over for coffee. I could not look at her face, her awful vulnerability. No one should love like that. And yet we do — we do.

I once heard a friend who was having a hard time with the man she loved, say to him, "I just want to follow you around like a dog." Our imagery gives us away. This same friend canoed in Nootka Sound by herself, slept out alone, ate alone by her campfire, for days and days. It's almost as though we have some kind of pre-frontal lobotomy when we women "fall in love." Eros' flaming arrow is really a scalpel which severs one part of ourself from another. And then, there we sit waiting for the words, "Rise up and follow me."

"He's almost thirty years old!" I cried.

She said later that she did not differentiate as far as love was concerned. Love was love, whether for an adult or a child or even an animal. I told her I thought that was crap, but later when I thought about love — and I think about it a great deal — I wondered if she wasn't right. If what we call "love" isn't based on some kind of reward/punishment thing. For the first time, I saw *you* (not just your ego) as the

109

dog and Hester as the master, the one with the food and the pats, the one who had the power to kick you out and let you in again.

What does the archaeologist do? He learns in schools and then he goes out on digs and, if he's inspired or lucky or goes down far enough, perhaps he "gazes on the face of Agamemnon." Literature, legend, drama comes alive in his hands. I wonder how such a one would reconstruct or interpret us, our shards? Was this Paradise or Bosch's Garden? How would they know? Supposing they found only your love letters to me, or mine to you. Supposing they did not find the overturned Christmas tree, the broken clay pot. Unless the disaster is so sudden and final (Pompeii, Knossos) that there is no time to tidy things up, right stools and pots, clear away the feast, get everyone back to bed, it's hard to be absolutely certain. The day after the Big Fight, the Christmas tree, still covered with bonbons and ribbons, was out on the curb for the dustmen. The pot it had stood in, broken beyond repair, had been swept up and put in the rubbish bin upstairs. The water had been mopped up. You and Hester had taken all your things and moved over to the Hotel Cleo. I went into the room across the hall. Only your rumpled sheets were there. You always checked every nook and cranny — even under the bed. You wouldn't have left anything behind. I gathered up the sheets, which were stained with your come marks, and took them upstairs to be laundered.

Tomorrow the women will walk to the baker's with their huge round pans of Sunday dinner. Later, the children will be sent to fetch them. The baker cooks no bread on Sundays and his old mother sits by the door and persuades unwary tourists to buy stale loaves at the regular price. "Kallimera," she says, "Kallimera." Most of the stale bread is made into a kind of melba toast (TOZT, I saw outside a cheap restaurant in Athens), which is very much fancied here. Nothing is wasted. Heleni's washing up water is poured on her little flower garden. Grapes are used to eat, the leaves as cases for "dolmades;" the stems as a base for ouzo. Goats provide milk and cheese. Olives are eaten or the oil pressed out. Even in that sophisticated city, Athens, as spring comes along, Athenian men and ladies wandered the paths of Philopappou Hill picking greens and herbs. An Englishman in one of the cafés the other night, eyeing the paper tablecloths, the plastic bread basket, said that modern Greece is becoming a nation of litterers. I said it was probably European and American influence. He felt it went much deeper. "The Greeks are accustomed, like most rural peoples, to making use of everything. Cans (unless used as flower pots) and plastic bags defeat them. The bag rips? It is just chucked into the nearest ditch or ravine. The whole concept of garbage is new to them." A cat, who was so thin its ribs showed through its ragged fur, sat under the table waiting for us to drop something.

"So, it is not boorishness, but a kind of despair which provokes them to litter?"

"I think so. And the landscape, as something to sit and admire, to be 'kept up,' is probably an alien concept too."

I went in one of those concrete "changing shelters" the other day, just to look. It was disgusting. Shit everywhere and tampax and sodden paper diapers. What prompts *that*? Who does it? Granted, there are no toilets on the beach, but Yannis has a toilet he'll let anybody use, and it's only a few minutes walk to his place. I think to myself, "Do the Greeks do this? Is this what's done on Sundays when all the families come?" It's appalling. Even Heleni, who strikes me as such a *spotless* person, always sweeping in front of the grocery store or hanging washing on the roof, lets her little grandson shit under that big tree across the way, the one where the donkey is tethered. And the flies come and land on her food or mine perhaps. Surely she understands the connection. This is not a street of squalor or degrading poverty. The men who are away in the towns bring money back to the women. Those that are here, Markos, his father-in-law the fisherman, the old man who mends saddles, all have trades and most have "Rent Rooms" as well. Why does Heleni let her grandson do this? Is it part of the same impulse that creates the filth of those changing shelters? And if so, what is it? It's not even a question of my being "over-fastidious," for I'm not. The bathroom of the Ramses Hotel in Latakia might revolt me, but I didn't insist that we move. It's just curiosity. Perhaps, because the boy is just a child, his toilet behaviour is ignored. But what of those big piles of adult shit behind that concrete shelter on the beach? That one was for ΓΥΝΑΙΚΩΝ, for "ladies." On the other hand, there is the bizarre lavatory in Herakleion, across from the bus depot. You found you couldn't even go, remember? One goes down some steps. ΓΥΝΑΙΚΩΝ, ΑΝΔΡΩΝ, whichever, and finds oneself in the same underground corridor. An old man (or an old woman, they seem to take turns) sits eating some fried fish at a small table. You hand him five drachmas and he goes and gets a few squares of rough toilet paper and the handle to a door. You follow and he inserts the handle, shows you in and shuts the door. It is quite clean and although one is peeing or shitting over a hole, there is a chain to pull and water to wash things clean.

You go back out and return the handle to him. He nods and continues his lunch. There is a dark-looking room beyond where they must *live*, where one of them must sleep while the other sits at the table. You said the old woman served you and you couldn't pee. You told me to stop laughing, it wasn't funny, and you disappeared to find a secluded wall, for we had a three hour bus ride ahead of us.

God, that place! To live down there. It was like something out of Victor Hugo. One expected the old woman to turn into a rat at any minute. I have used that washroom several times since, but I always flee as quick as I can up to the sunlight and the bustle of the cafés and vendors in front of the bus depot. I wonder how much money they make? I wonder if the city hires them or if it was their own idea. Hundreds, thousands of people take those buses in the season. At five drachmas a head (so to speak), a lot of money must pile up. But what a way to spend your life! When do they come up? When do they shop for the fish and meat and vegetables?

The guardians of the underworld have become an old man

and an old woman sitting in a public lavatory beneath the
city. I think I would be afraid to ask them their names!

"That man is following me everywhere." Or, as you say
in today's letter, the leopard aerogramme, "And so, you see,
you are with me for good, wherever you are. And I know I
am with you." You are sitting in your study in Africa writing
this. "It's nine p.m. The African night sounds outside. So
strange to imagine you back there in Aghia Sophia. Waiting
to hear from you," you write, "Love, Michael."

What part each of us will actually play in the other's
mythology remains to be seen. Already, I think you have
romanticized a relationship which, as you said in an earlier
letter, was really all-out war. I've told you before that there
were times I actually believed we might end up killing one
another. That's exhilarating for a while, that kind of "passionate intensity," but what we both knew was that it wore
us out, it got in the way of our "real" life, which is our work.
My love for my children does not affect me this way. It is
perhaps equally intense, but it is *permanent*, it is a constant
in my life and has been so for so long now that it is a part
of me — one of the best parts. If they withdrew their love
from me? Well, I don't know. I guess I can't imagine that.
Presumably, I would go on loving — that's what mothers do.
Maybe more than fathers, because it is their own *flesh*, their
own *blood* which is out there robbing banks or being elected
president. The visceral tie is very strong. Is that what Hester
with all her suppressed maternal instinct feels for you?
Almost the second time I met her, she said to me, "I don't
want any children." Later you said this wasn't so, that
it was you who didn't want kids. My own opinion as of
tonight, on this rooftop, is that neither of you wants them,
but for very different reasons. Is that what she meant?

Do you remember New Year's Eve, sitting for a few
minutes in Syntagma Square before we went down into
the Plaka? We started telling stories about previous New
Years' Eves.

"Last year," Hester said, "I read a magazine and went

113

to bed. My parents tried to cheer me up, but they couldn't. I couldn't make any conversation at all."

There was an appropriate silence. You looked at her very tenderly and repentantly. Then she told an interesting story. One New Year's Eve, I think after you two had been going together, but weren't yet married, you got very drunk at a party. "Let me kiss your lips!" you yelled to Hester, and then got down on your knees in front of her crotch. She went home.

You laughed and laughed as she told this — what a naughty boy you had been!

"Oh well," she said, laughing herself, "he was only nineteen."

"I must have been older than that," you corrected her, "you didn't know me when I was nineteen."

She excused you, Michael, by making you younger. And you loved her, sitting there in Athens telling this tale in front of you, to your (by then) ex-mistress.

I think that was one of the reasons, later on that evening, that I got up from the table and said I was going home. You had just suggested that you two walk me home via Philoppapou and we see the New Year in from the top of the hill. I thought, "I must get away from this couple. I am depressed sitting here knowing they are going back to the Cleo to cuddle up with one another and make love. I don't want to listen to any more stories out of their collective past. It's almost a New Year. I'll see it in alone."

"I think I'd like to go home by myself," I said.

"It's up to you," you said. Or "C'est à vous." You often used French expressions.

"I'm going to be alone very shortly," I said. "I think it would be unreal to see the New Year in together."

"I understand," Hester said.

"It's a symbolic act," I said. "I won't wait for the bill, I'll settle up with you later."

I went quickly out the door, half hoping that you'd run after me I guess. But of course you didn't. I began walking along Ariadnou a little way because I didn't like Athens alone at night. It was nearly twelve. More and more people were in the streets and then some bells began to ring. "CHRONIA POLLA," people called to me, "Happy New

Year." Couples kissed and there was a lot of laughter and jostling.

I made my way through the crowd and began to relax. Nobody was bothering me or following me. I could have been invisible. The moon was nearly full and as I came out of the Plaka, I decided to walk up the broad avenue of Dionysius Areopagite and home by that longer, but prettier way. The moon was up over the Acropolis, above and on my right. I was in Athens; it was a New Year. The security of your large presence beside me was gone — and gone, I knew even then, for good. I had blown up the ménage and it could probably never be attempted again. So what? I was in one of my brave moods. I was walking at my own pace, I was not running to catch up to you with your long legs. I knew my way home. I had been invited for a traditional dinner with my young landlady and her husband. It occurred to me as I walked along under the moon that Hester, who had now been in Greece for three weeks, was still unsure of the words for "please" and "thank you," and had not once ventured out on her own. You did that to her, this woman who, in reality, over the past painful year and a half, had become quite strong, quite independent. You were always there, leading the way, trying out your Greek, taking control. She was tired and emotionally upset and Athens was, indeed, scary for a woman alone. But I watched over the three weeks, it was as though you were some kind of whirlpool and she was being sucked back in. A horrible image, it's true, but that's what came to mind. She was not good at languages, she said; she didn't know the city. And yet in Paris, it had been the same. She never had a chance to try her French, she told me, you had your mouth open first. So many little "anecdotes" came out, Michael, during that three weeks. You had painted your life with Hester as ideal — and I suppose it was, from your point of view. From hers? Well, that's a different story. And yet each anecdote would end with some excuse or other — "He was confused," "He was young," "He's a Romantic," "He's so much better at those things than I am," "He was stoned."

I went home. I could hear revelry upstairs in the main part of the house, but I unlocked the door to my entrance and went in and went to bed. My alarm clock had stopped so I did not know what time it was. But it was a New Year. The Parthenon, amazing survivor, was up there on the hill. Once again I thought, "I have money and a room of my own and there's no excuse, now, not to be writing fiction." Just before I fell asleep, I wondered how you would have settled the New Year's kiss as we sat at the top of Philoppapou and heard the bells ring out. You would have had an arm around each of us, of course, but you could not possibly have kissed us both at the same time. It was just as well I walked away.

You brought my trunk up to Athens when you came. We made love; we went out to breakfast; we talked. You said it was "a new beginning." You said that you were very optimistic, that my letter and a letter from Hester had convinced you that it was possible to work things out. You had sent Hester a cablegram, you said, advising her of the new arrangements. You were very proud of the way you had phrased it.

"How was that?"

" 'The Sun Rises in Athens'," you quoted.

I "insisted" you have a few days alone with Hester, as she had originally requested. I even suggested the Cleo, "my" original hotel. It was clean and comfortable and the old man in the taverna next door played wonderful songs on his guitar. It was just minutes from the Acropolis, I said, just seconds to the shops in the Plaka or, in the other direction, Syntagma Square. I took you over to see it. You would have thought I was a bloody tour director or travel agent, I was trying so hard to please. After you two had some time to be alone, we would all three get together, travel together — maybe Turkey — live together.

I was feeling very strong and very good. I had a place to live, found by myself with no help from you, and I was beginning to know my way around. You teased me, but gently. "Just give me a map and a couple of days," you said.

I took you to the taverna next to the Cleo. I even dressed up in my new dress.

"Is that your boyfren'?" the guitar player asked.

"Yes," I said. I advised you on what to order.

"Hester will love this," you said. But I didn't want to talk about Hester anymore. Fuck Hester. She was still three days away. I ordered another pitcher of retsina.

"I love you," I said, "and I've missed you, and I'm willing to try a little harder."

"I've missed you too," you said. (But nothing about trying harder.)

"Well, even if we try it," I said to you that night in Aghia Sophia, "it won't be a ménage à trois for long; when we go back home, it will be a ménage à six."

"I've never considered living with your children again," you said.

"Then what are we talking about?" I said. "What on earth are we talking about?" I began to cry.

("He lives in a fantasy world," Hester said. "I knew this was just another of his fantasies.")

One of the Southern Ladies had enormously swollen legs and they literally had to be lifted, one by one, from the ladder and set into the tender. The fellows in the boat signalled you to help. You said you hadn't been so repulsed in years. Those huge legs with their varicose veins and the thick, clumsy body of Mrs. Whitelaw attached to them. I asked if you had no compassion for people growing old and you said it was possible to grow old without becoming gross and ugly.

"If one is lucky. She has run that grocery store by herself for years and years. It's affected her legs."

"She's just a big fat stupid ugly woman. All the people on this boat are stupid."

"They're lonely; their lives haven't worked out the way they might have wished. They've stopped thinking and

117

feeling. But I like Mrs. Whitelaw for her guts to even come on such a trip, and her friend for coming with her."

"They are utterly stupid women."

"Oh well, someday you'll be old."

"I'll be a very handsome old man."

"You have no sympathy for other people, Michael — and no empathy. How are you going to write if you can't get outside yourself?"

"*You* don't."

"I do."

"You do not. Your books are absolutely self-centred. And I think that's one of their great strengths."

"I think it's perhaps a weakness. But the point is, I *can* write about other people, I just don't choose to."

"So you say."

"So I know."

"Prove it. You can never even see *my* point of view, even after living with me so intimately."

"I can see it; I just don't happen to agree with it."

"Ha, ha, very funny." You raised your arm in a much-menacing gesture.

End of discussion, then. But Michael, you cannot stand to look at pain, sickness, death, decay or failure. But isn't it only when we become aware of our own mortality that we begin to create anything good? Art is merely the organization of *that* knowledge, *that* look at chaos. You saw my books — the objects — and were jealous and resentful. As though the finished product had not somehow been earned! How do you know what pain, what loneliness, went into those books?

I *understand* your repulsion for Mrs. Whitelaw. She is physically repulsive. When I was a child, my mother used to take us to visit some old relative or semi-relative named Mrs. Adams. She had phlebitis and edema and her huge legs, encased in grey stockings, were propped out in front of her on a footstool. They looked like elephant's legs. I was repelled and fascinated. My mother said they were full of water. I wondered if I stuck a pin in, like I did sometimes to birthday balloons, would they collapse and shrivel up and all the water puddle out on the carpet? I had all the awful curiosity and cruelty that only a young child, still unaware of the processes of decay already begun in her own body, can have. You are a man. You must get over this. Both for reasons of common humanity or, if that does not appeal to you, because you are an artist. The artist looks at everything, turns away from nothing, *cannot* turn away. In fact, a story could be written by you about your disgust. What it says about you, your fear of your own death. But you would have to understand why you were so disgusted.

Tell me, Michael, when you were helpless and ugly and unable to walk and shitting and peeing all over the place to boot, did your mother turn away from you? Why do we find that easy to deal with in babies (Or is it only that women find it easy, that women do not turn away in disgust?) and so hard to deal with in someone like Mrs. Whitelaw? The heroic act was not yours − grabbing and re-placing those swollen legs − it was hers. She had to trust you and the sailor. Why don't you write a story about it, Michael: the others in the front of the tender, fanning themselves with their hats, making cruel remarks; the Widow with her blue eyelids, standing next to me, up above where I was waiting to go down the ladder, saying people like that shouldn't be allowed to go on these trips (She herself was not planning to get off today; she had had "a little too much sun" the day before); Edna-Mae in her big straw hat and white gloves, holding her friend's purse, anxious for her, yet eager to get to shore − you could see it on her face; the harbour at Latakia with its hundreds of ships waiting to be loaded or unloaded; the heat; the fighter jets screaming overhead − the little boat, the tender, as some kind of metaphor maybe, I don't know − it's your story. Something would have to happen though − I leave it to you.

And if, according to Graves, "Blind Homer" turns out to be clear-eyed Nausicaa?

Perhaps when Hester got the job and announced that she was leaving for Africa in August, it was as though *she* were closing the account (to get back to my bank metaphor). Although the previous year, even though you had invested in me, she was there to draw upon. Your girlfriends weren't going to be transferable if you didn't watch out. What to do?

You came to me at one point.

"I can't go to Greece with you, Rachel."

"You're not going 'with me'; we're going together."

"You know what I mean." You were fighting back the tears. "Don't you see that saying 'yes' to you is saying 'no' to Hester?"

"I don't see. I thought you said 'no' to Hester, in that sense, a year ago."

You wept; we made love; I told you that we were both under a terrible strain, had been and would be until we got on that freighter and had some time alone together. You said you loved both of us, you'd just begun to realize it. I said that you would have to solve that one yourself. Then I began to cry. (Ours was certainly a relationship remarkable for its liquidity!) "Hush," you said. "Hush. Nothing is settled yet, nothing is settled."

And after one of these scenes, we would shove it all aside the next day, go to work on our own writing, hope that somehow it would all work out.

And then you came home after a night at the Aquatic Centre with Hester and as you undressed you announced, quite casually, that she had invited you to visit her in Africa. She would even pay your way down if you couldn't swing it. It was at that point that *I* began to panic.

Do you really like it down there, Michael? I know you say you are going home because Hester hates the people at the school (and they sound legitimately hateful) and that you need to get back to your "roots." But you are the world's greatest rationalizer. Do you like it there? Have you gained as an artist by going? You say so, but I'm not sure. You do not describe things to me very much; I get little sense of "Africa" from your letters. But maybe that's just because you are getting smart? I am, after all, your "rival." Why tell me what the "African night sounds" are that you were listening to when you wrote that letter. Why describe the streets to me in detail? If Hester wants to paint them, that's different. (But supposing she paints them better than you can describe them?) I'm not going to tell you — except in this imaginary monologue — that the priest's mother rings the bells. I read you out a letter I had written about Naples, do you remember? We were sitting at a café in Nicosia. I was showing off and you knew it. You were right to object, to tell me you did not want to hear any more descriptions of our shared experiences, especially not from someone as observant and articulate as I was. You were both admiring and angry. At the same time, you were surprised that I had been so frightened in that city. I tried to explain then that our shared experiences would be described differently, even the actual settings. But you were right; it's dangerous to be generous with one's observations. And I am a magpie; I pick up information whenever I can get it. (Do you remember the name of that café in Nicosia, the name of the street, the sky-blue berets of the U.N. troops, for example — that could be a very nice touch, or the dress of the old Egyptian woman at the hotel who told us in French that we could be shot if we went too near the Turkish zone?)

Our half-assed Greek lessons at night school at least enabled us to sound out a lot of the signs. It became a game on the bus up from Limassol. But our vocabulary was so limited that, in the end, we didn't really know what the word meant. As you pointed out, when Emily was learning the phonetic alphabet in Grade One and she sounded out APL, for instance, once she had sounded it correctly of course, she understood "apple" and knew what the word signified. But supposing she could not make the connection? Like a blind person learning a language, I suppose. Some were easy, however. At a gas station: ΠΕΤΡΟΛΙΝΑ = petrol = gas. (We were wrong, but didn't know it then.)

In English, outside an army base: FORBIDDEN AREA. NO PHOTOGRAPHS.

It was so hot in that hotel — hot and noisy. Each confessed to the other the next morning that he/she had felt like making love, but it was just too hot. Do you have that trouble down in Africa, Michael? Oh no — you have an air conditioned bedroom, I remember.

The scenes from that freighter trip remind me of poems,

not prose. The sense of quick, intense glimpses into the very essence of a city or town. The whore in the checkered shorts at Las Palmas, the row of headless statues in the Forum and that single yellow rose growing by a broken foot. The intense colours of the flowers and birds along Las Ramblas in Barcelona, and the old man who looked like Picasso asleep at the next table. The waiters with their white coats. The mound of clay pots beside the road in Cyprus, looking just like the clay pots in the Bible Scenes to Colour I'd taken home each Sunday as a child.

There was no expansion, no continuity, in and out — two days at the most. And yet I felt something in each place; I don't regret it. Most of the places (with the exception of our Roman holiday, all) were ports and so had *that* in common. Sailors and transients and the sea itself. But Las Palmas was very different from Naples, which was very different from Limassol and so on. Always moving East, of course, and farther into landscape and language which was more "Other."

And then there was Latakia.

If I were to write a novel about you, Michael, perhaps I would begin it thus (à la Conrad): "There are certain men of whom, by their extraordinary appearance, or from whom, because of their extraordinary appearance, the world is led to expect extraordinary things. Michael O'Brien was such a man, tall, with a large eagle-like nose, a rich full beard and a mass of dark wavy hair. But his height and darkness were as nothing compared to his eyes, which were of a beautiful shade of brown, speckled with green, and a most peculiar shape — oval and slightly slanted — like the eyes of a wolf. He looked like Rasputin perhaps, or a young sheik. He was, in fact, a poor boy from Québec and did not hesitate to tell you so. And if you met him at a party, or in a bar, it was not long before he would admit that he was a writer, a novelist, and his books were going to set the world on its tail. But he laughed as he said it, and somehow you both believed him and forgave him. "X" thought he was the most fascinating man she had ever met."

Near the base of the hill above the pier, there is a sentry-box. Left over from the Germans, I suppose. That's where you used to go to smoke dope at the end of your working day. You would climb the hill for exercise and then come down, light up and stand in the sentry-box, staring out to sea. You always went alone because you said you needed that time to "cool out" before we met for our swim. You would knock on my study door to let me know you were leaving. I would finish up what I was doing (towards the end, what I was actually *doing* was staring at the wall or writing my name over and over again, with variations) and get up and do the dishes left over from breakfast and lunch. That was pretty easy, as we always had the same thing: boiled or fried eggs for breakfast, with fresh bread and jam and coffee; and packaged soup for lunch, with more bread. I put water on to heat in a big pan and got into my bathing suit, put my trousers back on, washed up, packed my pack with mask, snorkel, towel, book, money and sweatshirt, as it grew colder. Then I walked down to the square and sat on one of the turquoise benches by the fountain and waited for you to join me.

You were usually quite excited, quite high, by the time you came down. Not really on dope, but on the sensation of a day's work done, more progress on your novel. We walked across the square, you talking and gesturing wildly with your beautiful hands, explaining a point or an insight. You were much more involved with writing as a craft than I was and it was very interesting to me to hear you talk about the "arrangements" you were making. I have never studied writing as a craft, in any abstract way I mean, although I sincerely believe it to be one. That does not mean to say that when I read I am not very aware of how the writer is drawing me in here, setting up a scene there, etc. But I seem only to be able to see it or analyze it in someone else — after it's been done. I once went shopping for a blouse with a friend of mine who sews and tailors beautifully. I would say, "That's pretty, I like that one," and she would turn it inside out, show me how badly it had been put together, where the maker had skimped, etc. She said it made her furious to see the kind of money people would pay for sloppy work. Well, it's a bit different with art, of course, since it's all done with mirrors, it's all illusion. There is no blouse on the page in front of you — I have to make you think there is. I have to make you believe that the temperature is pushing ninety and the sunlight bouncing off the white cubes of houses makes you squint. (I have to make you believe in the Emperor's New Clothes.) But the principle is perhaps the same. A good seamstress, like my friend, one who understands fabrics and darts and interfacing, can put together a blouse that is not only beautiful, but also well-made. After a while, that probably becomes intuitive — one no longer needs patterns — or one makes one's own. I don't know what stage I'm at, but I don't worry as much about "arrangements" as you do. This may be sheer laziness on my part or just greater faith in the material, that "negative capability" idea. There were times, crossing the square, walking under the cliffs to the beach that we preferred, that I felt perhaps your critical awareness would be your undoing, that the material dictates the form; you can't impose it. What happens to the tightrope walker if he stops to look down or even think about where he is? He trusts his feet, his body, to do that kind of "thinking" for him.

"Ah yes," you will say, "but writing is an intellectual exercise — the analogy is ridiculous." Is it, Michael, is it? I think you write with your whole body, that it's more a question of "balance" than you realize. (I do not mean mental stability, by the way.) At any rate, I would listen to you and marvel. I loved you terribly at those moments for you were so confident, so *sure* that you had found answers, keys, solutions. *Nothing* would stop you now!

If there were breakers, as there were towards the end, you would plunge in, enjoying the challenge of the waves. (While I, "tightrope walker" in my work, hung back, afraid when presented with The Real Thing.) Once, I cried because I was ashamed of being afraid and you came out of the water and said, "Come, take my hand, we'll go back in together." (I loved you so much at that moment!)

We would get out, dry ourselves and head for our afternoon ouzo and the mail.

"Someday I'd like to go up on the mountain with you," I said. "I want to see what the square and the sea look like from up there."

124

"I was writing Hester about it the other day," you said. "I was telling her how much she'll love it up there. She'll love the whole village. I'm really looking forward to the three of us sitting here after our swim and talking."

"I'm not always going to cook the evening meal," I said. "I refuse to cook every night for three adults."

"You'll say anything to start an argument, won't you? I'm sure Hester won't mind doing some cooking, she's an excellent cook."

"Good. Maybe we can take turns, all *three* of us."

"Get off my back, Rachel, will you?"

"Why don't we eat our evening meal out while Hester's here, then there won't be any arguments."

"You know we can't afford it — or she and I can't. It's costing her a lot of money just to come here, don't forget that."

"Ah yes, of course. But she's going to live free over the grocery store, isn't she? She gets the big room, you and I have to live and sleep in our studies."

"She doesn't have to come. I can still write and tell her not to come. I think you're just going to cause trouble. I can go down there right after Christmas as originally planned."

Why didn't I say, "Go then?" Why did I keep hanging on?

One of the husbands suggested that perhaps we should go and live with the hippies in the caves at Matala.

"Well, it would be a hell of a lot better than living in a pink ranch-style house in California," you said. He went pale and didn't speak to you for two days.

"Well," his wife said to me, "of course I understand what the *attraction* is, but Michael is so immachur."

If one sits on a blue bench under the huge tamarisk tree below Yannis' bar, under the tree made of green pubic hair — the pubic hair of mermaids maybe — if one sits there and stares across the couple of hundred yards of beach to the beginning of the cliff walk, it is better than a Fellini procession. A black-kerchiefed woman appears, riding her donkey; a tall blonde Norwegian girl in a bikini; two Greek soldiers on leave, looking very hot in their heavy wool uniforms; the pipe-maker, a sack full of pipes slung over his shoulder; a goat; Dog-Girl, with her dog; a group of Réthimnon widows who are staying in the village for a week and are down on the beach early (when I go first) and very late (when I go again). Sometimes I suspect they think I am a widow too, because I wear a one-piece black bathing suit and am not with any man. None of them can swim, but they stand in the water by the first beach, the pebble beach, and hold hands and laugh like little girls. They spray each other with water as well, and then all come out together and sit on the beach like a group of wise old blackbirds and watch the Europeans. They even wear their kerchiefs in swimming. I wonder if they are sisters. I will have to ask them. Already, they greet me every morning, "Tea-kán-ees, tea-kán-ees?" and offer me cookies, or toast which seems to have been fried in oil.

And then who? More bronzed bodies, more women on donkeys, the Sad Lady (a fairly new addition). One could easily imagine what Fellini would do with this, for it is only at the instant that you round that final corner that you really "come upon" the square with all its bustle. Again, a wonderful beginning for a movie.

The Sad Lady is pale as a forest mushroom and always alone. She walks very carefully, as though she were holding herself together. Perhaps she is recovering from an illness or an operation. She has been here about six days now and I have never seen her talk to anyone or go down to the square at night. She looks so sad — almost stunned. It is so *primary* here: the heat which increases every day, the brilliant sunlight, the sexual energy of the young tourists, the intense blues, greens, aquamarines of the sea. I wonder if this is such a good place to come and recover? The heat does strange things to people, strips away things that are essential to certain of us. I picture her sitting in a cool "shirtwaist dress," the kind we wore in the fifties and which are still advertised in *The New Yorker*, on a shady verandah, sipping an iced drink. Here, she wears a white Indian-cloth shirt over her bathing suit and a large purple towel wrapped around her waist. She has good ankles, but she has varicose veins. Where does she come from? What does she do in the evenings? She must be at one of the classier hotels up at the top of the road. Maybe she sits and reads. Maybe she writes love letters. Maybe she came here years ago with someone. Maybe she is dying. I can't guess what her nationality is — her hair is dark, but her skin is very pale. I would say she is American — that big luxurious bath towel, for example.

I wonder what they say about me here? Strange to think that I may be an object of speculation. Yannis remembers that I was here with you, and of course everyone on this street knows and has been informed by Heleni (who knows better) that my "husband" is down in Africa, working. I don't suppose I'm particularly interesting to the other tourists. Most of them don't stay very long anyway. But perhaps I will turn up in someone else's memories, or at the edge of a snapshot of Zorba's Bar. I suppose I should go around getting my picture taken with all the locals to use for the backs of future dust jackets. Me deep in conversation with the old saddle-maker, for example, a couple of saddles placed artistically outside his small white house. Riding a donkey perhaps. Whomping an octopus with all the fishermen looking on.

The only Greek picture of you and me, Michael, is when we sat between the sacred bull's horns at Knossos and asked that sailor to take our picture. It's quite nice of both of us and, looking back, highly symbolic. I included a copy of that one in the birthday album I gave you at your advance birthday party in Athens. I also included that very pretty one of me sitting at the far beach with nothing on but my floppy hat. It's quite decorous; my breasts show above my bent knees and my skin is a lovely colour against the sand. You wrote that you had got out the album on your birthday and looked through it. When I gave it to you, in front of Hester in Athens, you very quickly skipped over the picture of me naked except for my hat. Mumbled something about, "The far beach where we sometimes went on Sundays." *Sometimes*, Michael? We went there every Sunday afternoon and immediately took our clothes off and swam and had a picnic. We didn't *fuck* there. Anyway, you have a thing about

fucking outside. You don't seem to like it very much, perhaps because you are afraid of being interrupted, perhaps
because you feel, in that situation, so defenceless. However,
I wanted to embarrass you; I wanted Hester to think that
we did fuck here. It was all over by that time. Big talk about
me joining you two on holiday in Africa, but I knew better
— or I knew, shall we say, that I would come, if at all, as
"friend" and not as lover. You wouldn't want to lose Hester
again. I wasn't surprised when the erotic letters stopped and
all the various excuses as to why we'd have no time together
began. We had all pretended to be modern and liberal and
really, we are all old-fashioned and jealous and possessive.
Hester hides it better than you or I do — in some ways, she
is the most sophisticated, although both you and she would
claim she is the least. I was thinking the other day how well
she understands you, and how I would describe her if I were
using her in a story or a novel.

"Hester O'Brien was one of those small, soft-spoken,
utterly determined women, whom more flamboyant creatures like myself inevitably underestimate."

She told you I had gone to the seminar "looking for a
man."

It was not true and you knew it; but the seeds were
sown in the moist earth of your already jealous soul.

She said, "I give it six months."

She said, knowing how determined you were to say you
had "made it" (when you did), without any help from
anyone at all (especially a woman), "Rachel can further your
career for you in a way that I never could."

I don't mean that these remarks were necessarily calculated, but they had a certain brilliance. And I *had* seen
other men in the seminar, even when I began seeing you.
You were married — I had not intended to break up your
marriage. You had some crazy idea at that point that I would
be faithful to you alone, while you remained "faithful" to
Hester *and* to me.

I wonder if there are lots of crimes of passion on this
island? Those sharp, glittering Cretan knives always seem

128

available here. And women are most certainly "possessions." But do the women ever kill their husbands for fooling around? I don't think my vocabularly is up to asking Heleni that. Maybe Yannis will tell me.

Hester had written that she wanted a week alone with you in Athens before Christmas.

"A week? I thought you were just going up to get her."

"Look, Rachel, we agreed on no sex, any of us, while we were together. But she and I haven't seen each other in months now. She's very tired and nervous — we can both see that from the letters she's sent. She's asked for time alone with me. That's only natural."

"Athens was where *we* were going together, it was going to be *our* special Greek treat."

"We've been through all that. I can't fucking well afford two trips."

"I didn't know you were going to turn picking up Hester into a Dionysian orgy. I think that's unfair."

"You can go anytime — this may be the only chance I get."

"I wanted to go with *you*!"

"That's impossible. We've rehearsed all this before; you're making me tired."

"*You're* making *me* tired. You get me to agree to you going up to Athens to pick her up and now it's going to be a weeklong holiday. I think that's a dirty trick — on both your parts."

"You don't know how to share, do you? You're just a fucking jealous possessive bitch."

Later, she begged you to come down in time for her birthday.

"You said that if Hester came here for a month, you would stay until March."

"I never said how long I'd stay."

"You did. You said, 'for two more months.'"

"I don't remember saying that."

"Well, you certainly never put it down in writing, you were very careful."

129

"She feels bad about spending her birthday alone down there. It's her thirtieth, after all. It's rather special."

"My birthday's special too; all birthdays are special. I wanted to go for a holiday in Athens. Hester has more or less said that I can't do that — rather more than less. Now I'm saying she can't have you in Dar on her birthday."

"You can't tell me what to do."

"I can tell you to GET OUT!"

"Is that what you want? I'll get out. Or you get out. You're the one who's causing all the trouble. I can't work with all this fucking nonsense going on."

I stripped my bed and went to sleep in the study. I told myself, once again, I was a lunatic, weak-willed, a fool to put up with these manipulations. In the middle of the night, I got up and got the coffee pot so you wouldn't be able to make coffee. I was supposed to make it anyway. You got up every day and ran down the hall to put it on; I went and got it and served it. We sat in our beds drinking coffee and eating cheap biscuits. It would still be dark outside, and very quiet.

I heard you get up and go down the hall. (I'd taken the coffee and all the cups as well.) You stormed into my room.

"Please knock," I said sweetly, "you know the rules."

"Do you want me to leave, is that it?"

You looked so funny, standing there in your too-small T-shirt and nothing else. You looked like some kind of bird.

"It's my coffee pot. If we're going to be so *possessive*, we might as well go all the way."

"Get up and get us some coffee, you bitch."

"Well — I was about to make *myself* some. In a few minutes. When I get up the energy. I didn't sleep too well last night. If you're in a hurry — hmmm. I wonder what the fishermen do? Perhaps the καφenéon is open early."

"If you don't get that coffee to me in ten minutes, I'm leaving."

Later, we talked. I told you that I could not help feeling jealous. I wanted to do something with you that would involve a few days of no work and lots of play. I said I was hurt because Greece was our trip, yours and mine, and I resented you being in Athens with Hester — that it was more than sexual, that it was as though you had taken back my

130

birthday present and given it to her. I cried. I said I didn't want you to leave. I said I didn't want you to cut me out of your life.

You were very forgiving. You promised me we'd have a really lovely time in Herakleion, spend the night in a hotel, and you'd even buy me my birthday dinner. (A joke about your insistence that everything be split down the middle, to the very last cent.) You said that you loved both of us and you wanted to be fair to both of us. And somehow, the subject of you going down to Dar by Hester's birthday wasn't mentioned again. I knew you'd go. I knew by then that you'd do anything she told you to.

Soon you were merrily tapping away in your study again.

Perhaps I am, after all, the real villain(ess) of this piece. I pretended to be someone I was not. I pretended to you, to Hester — and worst of all — to myself. I could *never* have given you what you wanted, and every time you recognized this and were ready to leave, I would cry, "No, no, I'll be good. I'll try harder. I *can* make you happy." And it wasn't true. I wasn't good. I never tried harder. I didn't budge one inch. I did not want your arrival in my life to involve *me* in any changes or compromises at all. I knew who I was and where I stood and you would have to be the one to do the accommodating. To Hester, while I was still the "Other Woman" and not the "Wife," I tried to appear generous, tolerant, liberated, totally unpossessive. No — even before I was "officially" the "Other Woman," that's how I wanted to appear. I do think the ménage might have worked (I know I broke it up), because a part of me doesn't want a full-time husband at all. For three years, my energy had gone into my relationship with my children and my books. It was like a reverse Parkinson's Law. I had contracted my focus — a husband was no longer part of it. Then I fell in love with you, and somehow, I could not expand again. And you, of all people! Of all the worst possible types for me to fall in love with. My marriage had been fourteen years of relative calm with my husband, in many ways, playing Hester's role — the Calm One, the Steadier. It was a very comfortable arrangement (for me). I loved him; I bore his children. I depended on him for support. He got bored and walked away — he wanted Romance, Passion; maybe just more warmth and attention. I don't think I started to grow up — as a separate human being — until he walked away. I hated you for all your weaknesses because they had been mine. And I was not willing to be your Traditional Wife anymore than you were willing to be my Traditional Husband. All your final talk of responsibilities towards and commitments to Hester was nonsense: you missed her and would not live without her commitment and responsibility towards *you*. I know the feeling; I recognized it in you. I wonder, sometimes, what would have happened if we had broken up, Hester had gone for good and you had had to face living with yourself? When was the last time you *really* did something on your own, Michael? I had planned to go to Greece before I met you; it was Hester's idea to go to Africa. For nearly ten years, with the exception of two weeks alone in Aghia Sophia (and then you had two women writing you constantly, desperately in love with you), you have had a woman by your side — especially during any "adventure," anything new. Your one day in Addis Ababa, you went to bed at seven p.m., utterly overwhelmed by what you had seen. I'm not *blaming* you, Michael. I'm just suggesting it must have been awfully nice to see Hester's familiar (loved) face at the airport in Dar.

You talked a lot about "taking risks." You're a very good poker player; you won a lot of money off those fellows on the ship. I think you take calculated risks; I think you make sure you cover your bets. So how did I get from me as villainess to you as villain? I'm not sure — you always did tease me about my logic. And it's so comfortable sitting here alone, drinking retsina and scolding.

In one of the letters you wrote, you said, "You talk of being 'totally committed' to me but, my love, you have three children. Circumstances tower and crash. Love does not conquer all." I wonder if you and Hester will get a puppy when you settle down, back in Montréal, or if you will have a child. A puppy would be so much easier. Poseidon's wife turned one of her competition into a dog, I seem to recall, but that's another story. It had six heads. You wouldn't want anything as attention-getting as that. Just a cute puppy with whom you could go on walks in the rain. And then, if you decided to move, it could aways be given away or put to sleep. But I don't know, if the child were your own and not someone else's, I think you might love it a lot. You are extremely territorial, as you well know. Does Hester want a child? I never figured that one out. I think not, but then I think that half the time she just says what she thinks you want to hear. "You feel the absence of your children," she said to me in Athens on Christmas Day, "I very much feel their presence." They had sent me drawings and prints and photographs, and I cried. After the turkey was collectively plucked by all the people staying in the house, the three of us went for a walk. The Acropolis was closed, but we took pictures of each other on the rocks just beside it. You and Hester, you and me, Hester and me. We had all slept in the same room, my room, on Christmas Eve; you on a mattress between the two beds. Everything was going swimmingly. Tonight, you would go across the hall to Hester's room, then it was your turn to sleep alone. We were very very organized and "realistic" about it all. Hester had confessed in Delphi that she had cried the first night that you and I had slept together with her under the same roof. But she'd get over it, she said, she was just being silly and grumpy. We were both very tender with her that day — she was so obviously tired and nervous — and her confession seemed to draw the three of us together. We were all going to have to be very honest about our feelings, we said, this is all so new. On the train back to Athens from Meteora, Hester sat with her head against your shoulder, her eyes closed, and I sat opposite you, your long legs stretched out across the seat, touching my thigh. From time to time, we smiled at one another as she slept and then we got into a curious conversation about the difference between male and female novelists and whether one of the essential differences was that men tended to set their stories clearly in an historical framework of fairly large proportions, whereas women did not. I suspected that this was a load of old horse manure, but Hester sat up, said she hadn't been sleeping, just resting, and that she thought that was probably true; compare *War and Peace* with *Pride and Prejudice*, for example. I nodded and smiled; I don't think I really cared about the discussion. We had made love the night before and you had asked me to suck your cock because you liked that so much. I liked it too, liked your whole beautiful body in the dim light of the tiny hotel room. Why couldn't it all work out, three mutually loving people, living together and helping one another grow. Why, indeed?

What about *Uncle Tom's Cabin*, I said, trying to pay attention? (I was massaging your foot.) What about *Mrs. Dalloway*? But I smiled as I said it. We were all smiling a lot in those days. The train rocked us slowly towards Athens.

Later that evening, I tried to find a particular little café near the Tower of the Winds. You were cranky and hungry; we were all pretty cranky and hungry. I felt that I really must find it and, for some reason, it seemed to have disappeared. You wanted to take us to another place. Hester intervened. It didn't matter where we ate, she said, she was so happy just to be eating Greek food and being in Athens. The next day, you pointed out how you and I had been on the brink of a fight, how Hester had prevented it and made us realize how silly we were being. You saw this as a good sign — great hope for the future. Poor Hester was going to be Mother to us all!

"What would you like for your birthday?" you said one day in Aghia Sophia.

"I'd like one of the little rings they sell in Crete. I don't think they're very expensive."

You picked up the plates to carry them to the kitchen. "No," you said, "no rings."

"Why not?"

"Because you are who you are."

I didn't know what you meant, but it sounded awful. Who was I that I couldn't have a cheap ring for my birthday? I went in my study and sat on the bed and brooded. Later, when I saw the drawing Hester did of your two faces and her rings — it was probably an anniversary present — the drawing which you accidentally left behind in a box of typing paper in Athens, I realized I had said exactly the wrong thing. Rings were for Hester, your wife. Then I worked myself into a terrible frenzy and we had yet another fight. You said, how did I know you weren't getting me a ring and you just wanted to put me off. I said you were putting me *down*, not off, and what did you mean? You didn't know what you had meant, it was just a casual remark. *You* ended up crying this time. You said that you had been sitting there thinking, *that* afternoon you would finally invite me to go up the mountain with you.

"You just want to make sure you get it in before Hester comes," I said, "so you'll be free to take *her* up there."

I couldn't leave it alone.

I couldn't leave "well enough" alone.

Every time I heard you talk about "sparing Someone's feelings," I knew that you were afraid to tell Someone the truth.

" Ἑλλάς, Ἑλλάς." GREECE. "ἡ Ἑλλάς." "Alas," "Alas," "Alas." That's what it *sounds* like. But no, I doubt if I'll ever think of it that way — the trip here, our stormy life together. As you used to write to me, borrowing your style, I say, "Hello, Michael, I love you." But only in my fashion. I love the fact that I've been hours alone on this rooftop, enjoying the shift from day to night, the freedom to stay up here as long as I choose — even to sleep up here. If it gets much hotter, and I understand it will, I think the children and I will be sleeping up here — all five of us, for Robert's coming too. He is "between friends" and restless. We can talk lying down and watch the stars. This is the longest the girls and I have ever been apart; I wonder if we'll feel strange at first. *Do* I love them the way Hester loves you? I like to see them growing up, becoming women, even though I know they grow apart from me by doing so. That may hurt, but it's inevitable. And I have to keep growing too, for my sake, as well as theirs. To be an example to them, yes, but also not

135

to die an early. spiritual death, like those sad people on the boat. In the end, it seemed to me that Mrs. Whitelaw and Edna-Mae, for all their *physical* handicaps, thick glasses, hearing aids, swollen legs, were more adventurous than others, more alive. The last night (our last night, for the ship was going on to Malta from Piraeus and then turning around to begin it's journey back to New York), Edna-Mae brought in her Memory Book for us to sign. I loved what you wrote: "To Edna-Mae, may you always get off at every port." She was really tickled. She offered to mail some inlaid boxes we'd bought for our mothers in Latakia. The boat would be back in the States in little over a month and it would be cheaper and more reliable than sending them from Greece. We will never see her again, I shouldn't think, or Mrs. Whitelaw, who is probably back behind the counter at her grocery store. The husbands made fun of them because they didn't have men with them (even though I pointed out that both were widows) and because they were so deaf. The Widow also thought they were pretty funny, she who sported iridescent blue or green eyelids, like some insect, and was afraid to leave the boat. And we made fun of them as well, albeit privately. We made fun of all of them, even the superior Professor and his wife.

Oh Michael, I will never forget Shay Weinstein sticking her head through the porthole and screaming up at you — "Michael, Michael! I'm trying to get some rest!"

And you, leaning over from the sun deck and screaming back at her, "Well, *I'm* trying to get to Latakia!"

I suppose that coming to me from Hester was like coming to a big city from a small town. You had left the familiar, tree-lined streets (where you had a definition, a name, the very thing I've been thinking about in terms of the people of Aghia Sophia, where you were loved for sure, and life had a certain order) for the bustle and excitement, yes, but also the loneliness and anonymity of the metropolis. Suddenly, you realized that it was *up to you* to amuse yourself, define yourself, etc. You and Hester had led such an enclosed life — emotionally, I mean. You had travelled a lot and worked in a lot of different places, with very few friends — because you were always moving — except each other. It was one of the things you kept saying after the break-up, one of the reasons you felt you had to keep in touch. You had "brought her" to Vancouver; you were "her only friend." As a matter of fact, you don't like the idea of Hester having intimate friends, do you? I think she fared/fares far better in the Outside World than you do. I think she is far more genuinely friendly, even if she *is* painfully shy. How can anyone who is as egotistical as you are have real friends? Real friendship involves equality. That does not mean I might not be superior to my friend in some ways, he/she to me in others.) Perhaps "mutuality" would be a better word. What you want is an audience. Hester maybe bends too far the other way; she's afraid to be anything but "audience" and that is why you suit each other so well. It's like the bird who lives on the back of the hippopotamus or the one that cleans the crocodile's teeth. Such intimacies are allowed because they are mutually beneficial. However, I'm damn sure these birds know that they could be crushed or swallowed at any time. Does this have to do with your preference for small women again? They may not be able to keep up with you when walking, but you can put up with that because they offer no physical threat. You could overpower either of us in a couple of minutes, unless we knew judo or karate. Most men can, physically, overpower most women. A big man like you must be very aware of that. I suppose you would say you like your women to be "feminine," not "fucking Amazons." And we, of course, are taught from infancy to "look up to" men, to be the "little woman."

Once when we were making love, I told you something I liked. You were hurt. You said, "Are you criticizing my technique?" I pointed out that you often made suggestions or told me about things you liked and I'd never thought of it as a criticism of *my* technique. Our bodies were new to one another, our particular preferences not necessarily known. You accepted this; I think it was the first time you'd ever thought about it. But your remark haunted me — "Are you criticizing my technique?" Did you think that because you had "solved the problem" for one woman, you had solved it for all? I couldn't believe that you were that naïve. You had known dozens of girls before you were married — surely, you must have noticed that some liked one thing; some another? And maybe the same girl liked something different on Tuesdays, different from what she liked on Mondays, who knows? You liked variety and made no secret of it. "Technique!" That *word*, even!

Another one of your phrases, that you wrote once or twice in a letter: "I'd like to fuck you into the ground." As though I were a fencepost or a nail to be hammered home. So violent. That one gave me pause.

And yet, in reality, you were a wonderful lover, and never violent, always tender and gentle. What you said and what you did were very different. You are such a *paradox*, Michael, such a complex person. One of the most sexual men I've ever met and yet always telling me to button up my blouse or not to touch people. Hester said once that it was amazing how you had no sexual hang-ups at all.

"Oh, I think he does."

"In what way?"

"He thinks sex is dirty or somehow forbidden. That's why he enjoys it so much. He likes to use that phrase a lot, 'Doing dirty things.' He's doing something his mother (most mothers) would never really approve of."

We giggled. Was it mean, Michael, to discuss you behind your back? To giggle at your long legs and how your old T-shirt only came to below your ribs? And yet you insisted on sleeping in a T-shirt. I suppose it was mean; I suppose that's why we did it. We knew you had discussed each of us with the other. We lay in our separate beds, with you in the other room and we giggled like a couple of schoolgirls.

By Christmas Eve, we had been racing around Athens for two days on "secret missions" and Hester and I had filled your stocking (which was so enormous that all the presents wouldn't fit), while you and I did hers, and you and she did mine. There were lots of people staying in the house, which was essentially a bed and breakfast place, and we had been to a costume party upstairs. We had gone as the Three Wise Men, dressed in bedsheets with bits of African cloth and you with the Arab headdress you had bought from the trader in Latakia. We carried long church candles which smelled of beeswax, had real incense and frankincense which we'd

138

bought at the street market, and had gilded walnuts. The day before, Hester had spotted a rather sad-looking artificial Christmas tree put out at the curbside up the street and we'd carried it home, shoved it in a big clay pot (for its base was gone) and decorated it with Greek cookies and candies.

There was a tree upstairs too, and wine and music, and we were all going to have a communal dinner the next day. The turkey, with its revolting head and feet on, still needing to be plucked and singed, reposed in the fridge. We did not tell anyone about the ménage à trois business — I think we knew they would laugh or look at us with incredulity. But it was working. One night with Hester; one night with me; one night Hester and I sharing a room while you slept alone. You, of course, were in the region of Seventh Heaven, or even higher, if there is one. You and I went off to get little things for Hester's stocking, you and she went off, then she and I. We also had all the stuff we'd bought at Herakleion on my birthday trip (the lovely white dress for Hester) and she had mysterious parcels she'd brought up from Africa. Your mother had sent us a wonderful food package and there was a large brown envelope from my daughters, saying do *not* open until Xmas morning.

I remember how excited I felt because we had finally been adult enough to work things out. There would be no "losers." Hester and I both loved you; we *could* learn to love one another. Now that she had begun to relax a little, I found her very warm and open and very candid about her own fears and hopes. I didn't seem to mind about the months you would be down in Africa with her alone. I had my book to do — at least the first draft — and I would join you after the girls went home in August. I'd come down for a month perhaps, in April, when Hester had her holidays. Maybe we could travel around a bit and see something of East Africa. We would all go back to Canada together.

I fell asleep very happy, only wishing that my children were there to make the happiness complete.

"Hey," you said, "I don't know about this business of being down here on the floor with you two ladies on beds up above me."

"It's where you belong," Hester said.

"I'm going to have to deal with *two* fucking bitches from

now on," you said, but you said it happily.
"Goodnight, Michael."
"Goodnight, ladies."
"Goodnight."
"Goodnight."
"Goodnight."

The other afternoon, when all the Beautiful Ones were sitting at Zorba's, stretched out in the blue chairs, drinking or playing backgammon, and Joni Mitchell was singing about the caves at Matala, suddenly there was a terrible commotion up on the rooftop over the bar. Yannis' mother appeared, like something out of the *Oresteia*, black-robed and screaming, and carrying a heavy suitcase. She heaved it up on the railing and flung it down into the crowd below. The English girlfriend's panties and bras and dresses flew out everywhere.

In my notebook I found a brief conversation I recorded one day on the freighter, when I told you my insides were upset:
1) "Oh *No*!"
2) "Jesus, I hope I don't get it."
3) "Are you taking the Lomotil?"
4) "Jesus, we'd better be careful you don't touch anything of mine."
5) "Jesus!"

But when it was good, Michael? When we sat up in bed half the night, talking about books, drinking wine, laughing, making love — nothing could touch it, maybe nothing ever will. I bought little bouquets of fresh flowers for upstairs and downstairs; I bought books for both of us to enjoy; I told you all the secrets of my heart and listened while you told me yours.
"We're so *intimate*," you said once, in wonder.

140

Sometimes we played silly games, like trying to figure out where each had been at a given moment in a given year. We figured out that you were twelve years old when I was giving birth to Hannah. I was a "grown-up;" you were even a "young man."

("O," I would think, *pray*, during the good times, "O, please God, let it last.")

"I can't stop loving you, Rachel," you wrote to me from Dar. "I miss you terribly. Am re-learning how very lonely writing is. And I worry about you. You're so *dumb*."

There was no beer left in the galley fridge. Just tonic, Collins mix, soda and ginger ale.

"No *beer*!"

"Shhh." (Except for dim nightlights, this whole end of the ship was in total darkness. Everybody was in bed except us, and we were stoned.)

"No *beer*." (Exaggerated whisper.)

"None."

"What about the carton of booze in the lounge?"

"We can't take any of *that*. It belongs to the boozers."

"Let's go see."

We lurched along to the lounge and tried to find the light-switch. First we lit up the corridor, then the stairs.

"Shh. Everybody will come after us. There's the carton."

You pulled out a bottle of gin. It was maybe one-third full.

"Let's have gin and tonics."

"Take the whole bottle?"

"Why not?"

I found a bottle of vodka, about as far gone as the bottle of gin.

"I prefer vodka tonight."

"Let's take both of them."

We tiptoed noisily out and had great difficulty turning all the lights off. The idea that we might be discovered just added to the general hysteria. We stopped in the bar for glasses and mixer.

"We can't sign for the mixer!"

"No — no, we can't." We looked at each other seriously. This was different; now we would be stealing from the *ship*.

"It can't be helped," you said. We more or less bounced off the walls, doubled over with laughter, reached our cabin and put the latch on the door.

We toasted ourselves, the moon, Teneriffe, Las Palmas, Barcelona, Genoa, Rome, Limassol, our absent friends, Hester, my absent daughters, our books, whatever we could think of. You taught me to say "Screw them," in Norwegian. POKKER I DEM.

And then, there was no more drink and we were very drunk and felt it was time to go to bed.

"What are we going to do with the bottles and cans?"

"?" You looked so completely non-comprehending, so puzzled, that I began to laugh again.

"The bottles and *cans*, dear. And the *glasses*. The chambermaids will find them."

"They'd never tell."

"Maybe not. But I wouldn't want to put them in that position."

"I know a couple of positions I'd like to put that Astrid in."

"Be *serious*."

"I am. Astrid, show me your cunt. What d'you think she'd say if I came up behind her and whispered that in her ear?"

"Listen, Michael, we have to get rid of the evidence. We've been stealing."

"They'll never suspect us; we hardly drink. By their standards, we're teetotallers. And they'll never suspect the Southern Ladies. That leaves each other! They'll suspect each other!"

We rolled on our beds, laughing.

"Come here, you."

"I will, I will, but what about the *evidence*?"

You sat up; you looked around; you smiled.

"The portholes!"

"The portholes! Of course."

We took turns throwing things out. Cans, bottles, glasses — everything, even the ashtray.

"We're littering the ocean. Maybe some poor fish has just been knocked unconscious. Maybe a mother fish, with babies to see to."

We stared out a porthole, looking down at the rushing water. I gave you a hug.

"Now I feel like something to suck," I said.

"What kind of thing?"

"Dunno. Any old thing, Something refreshing — a Popsicle."

"I'll give you something refreshing."

We undressed each other and crawled into your bed.

"The best thing," you said, "is that they *will* suspect each other."

"I won't be able to go for drinks at noon; I'll start to laugh."

"You always put in an appearance; you'll have to go."

"I'll laugh."

"No, you won't. You go and tell me all about it. I'll wander in late, as is my wont."

They never said a word to either of us. I was a bit late, and by the time I arrived, new bottles were in evidence. At first, we thought perhaps they didn't even miss the old ones, but that evening we noticed that relations were cool between the two couples and neither left their bottles in the lounge anymore.

As we threw the evidence out the portholes you yelled, "Take it, Jesus, take it!"

"We're going to be struck like lightning or run into a hurricane or one of those giant waves."

"Nonsense. The gods are always on the side of artists."

"Whoever told you that?"

"Don't question me, woman, just accept what I say."

Do you remember the money-changer's crippled son? I suppose he's got one of those diseases like multiple sclerosis which attack the nervous system. About a week ago, he started going swimming. He comes down to the square, the long way around because his father's shop is on the street with steps leading down to the square. He has a homemade go-cart affair, with a brake, and he comes down the other end of the street of the tavernas, past the tobacco kiosk, the kaφenéon and the grocery story where we used to shop, and into the street that the post office is on. Down that, towards the sea. He rounds the far end of the square, the pier end, and begins his journey across the square. People call to him, "Hey, Georgi, Tee-kán-ees, hey!" He smiles his sweet smile and keeps going, past the volleyball game, the big tavernas with their awnings, Zorba's, where bronzed legs are pulled back to make a path for him. "Georgi! Ya Georgi!" the fishermen shout. When he reaches the end of the concrete, one of the fishermen, or even one of the taverna owners, gets up from where he is sitting and comes down to help, rolling up his pants. Strong arms carry the crippled man across the sand and into the water. Once there, George can use his own strong arms and floats and swims a bit, turns over and floats on his back with a look of absolute bliss on his face.

The men sitting under the tamarisk tree keep an eye on him, without seeming to. Small children frolic around him. The pregnant woman from our street stands in the water in her dress, as her little ones splash wildly and do a lot of screaming. She smiles at the crippled man. "Hérete." "Greetings." When he has been in the water for about twenty minutes, one of the men, not necessarily one of the older men, sometimes a contemporary, comes down to the water again, lifts him out and holds him while another dries him a bit with a ragged towel. He is offered a drink, but he usually refuses. He is settled back into the go-cart and begins his arduous way home; everyone is pleased that he has had his swim. He must live in the back of the shop, or else he is carried up and down steep stairs every morning and evening. He cannot stand at all. Someone must clothe him, take his wet, old-fashioned woollen bathing suit off him, make sure he is really dry and put him in fresh clothes. There is nothing wrong with his intelligence. When the father is not here, he runs the store, selling stamps, suntan lotion, cookies, tampax, postcards, all the "touristy" things, and even changing money. Someone from the village is usually there talking to him and reaches up, if necessary, with a long hooked stick to get whatever is needed. He can talk — in Greek or in English

— but, very, very slowly. His face is not defeated or dull or angry, and somehow, perhaps with the help of his father (there seems to be no mother) and the rest of the village, he has been made to feel *essential* and loved. He contrasts sharply with Yannis, who has only his wine-splash birthmark to contend with — and obviously a lot of women besides myself don't find him unattractive, and yet he is angry and desperate. Is a minor handicap harder to take than a major? Georgi is so obviously "Other." Is it in some way *easier* for him? What does he think when the perfect young German boys come in to buy stamps in their sexy bathing trunks? As a Greek, nurtured on centuries of worship of physical perfection, especially in the male, can he admire them in some abstract way, as he might admire the Boy of Marathon or the famous Poseidon? Or does it hurt? What are his dreams like? What does he dream about? I go in there to buy stamps for letters to the girls; to my friends; to you, still both more and less than friend. I like to put different stamps on and will make up seven drachmas for a postcard in all kinds of elaborate ways. He doesn't care. He opens the big book of stamps and tears them off one by one. His father changes my money and gives me a sesame cookie. I can buy stamps at the post office, of course, and I often do, but I also like to buy at the money-changer's shop.

"You write a lot of postcards," the father says, smiling.

"I write a lot period. That is my profession." "Εἶμαι ἡ συγγραφεύς." I'm not sure I've said it right. "Biblio," I add. "Book."

The boy's slow voice comes out.

"You . . . write . . . books."

"Yes."

After this, they always ask me how my books are coming.

Michael, what have we lost, as human beings, by massing ourselves in cities? It frightens me. It frightens me that my daughters, thousands of miles away from grandparents, know nothing of old age — both the joys and the sorrows. It frightens me that we lock away or shunt to "special schools" anyone who is physically or mentally different. We are producing a society as perfect and smooth on the surface as any other good plastic. We are bad Samaritans and we turn the other cheek only because we are anxious to look away.

We lock up suffering, like Rochester's wife, and hope she won't bother us. We will call her Grace Poole and deny she is one of our own.

How about this, Michael? "He now lives in Montréal, Québec, with his wife, Hester (to whom he gives full credit for typing his manuscripts, checking grammar and providing moral support), and a German shepherd named Sinner Man." No, that won't do. Hester, thank God, refused to learn to type on principle and you consider yourself an authority on grammar. Let's see. How about just, "To Hester, my wife." And later, "Once again, to Hester." She's right. When you appear on talk shows, you will be wonderful with your thick dark hair, your black beard, your fine eyes. You will laugh and gesture and talk on and on about Miller, your inspiration, and Joyce, your exspiration, and your roots, and all the things that, indeed, you talk about so well. They'll have difficulty shutting you up and going on to the woman who gave birth to seven children at one time.

And will the camera pan in and then away, and will we catch a glimpse, just for a second, of your long legs in trousers that somehow are too short? Will you still be wearing blue jeans and a sweater — The People's Novelist — or will you be having your suits custom-made by then?

Will you mention immediately that you are happily married and have been so for many years? Will I, will "us," be erased from your official biography? It would be easy to do (providing I keep quiet).

And what if we meet at some party, in Toronto, say, several years from now? It's a big party, maybe in your honour — no, maybe it's in somebody else's honour — and we just happen to be there. Our hostess, who is one of those vaguely literate types who offer to "open their homes" for such occasions, brings me forward to meet you, or you me. Neither of us has become a superstar, but we each have our own solid reputations and adequate following. The hostess, of course, knows our names, but has not read any of our books, because we aren't that important. She takes me, like a small child, by the wrist and leads me forward.

146

"Michael, do you know Rachel?"

There is an amused silence amongst THOSE WHO KNOW. For of course you are the black-bearded villain of my most recent novel and I am the red-headed villainess of yours. Hester is standing beside you, looking very pink-cheeked and pretty.

"Hello, Rachel."

"Hello, Michael. How nice to see you. Hello, Hester." There's just one thing I'm not sure of: whether you are really as good as you think you are. I can't tell, or I can no longer tell. I haven't seen the final draft of your novel and I'm a poor critic at the best of times. You have a faith in yourself that is very contagious. You will therefore probably "succeed," whatever that means. But you don't want "just" to succeed. You want reputation as well as fame. Who knows whether you will get it or not? I try to imagine what your life will be like if the one dream you've had for most of your life doesn't come true. I try to imagine Hester's life with you. What would you do with your life? I think again of Conrad, of *Lord Jim*: "A man who is born falls into a dream like a man who falls into the sea." It could all end in disaster. Robert has said that the real reason I fell in love with you, aside from the great physical attraction, was because I knew in my heart you were no threat and that the reason you left was because you knew it too. No threat as a writer, he meant. Is that true? I denied it vehemently and became a veritable Hester, as I pointed out to him your comedy, your dialogue. Then I hear myself overpraising you, the way you overpraise Hester, and I wonder. Even in your most angry moments, you never ceased being a great admirer of mine, so perhaps I feel I "owe it to Michael" to reciprocate. Fuck it, who cares. I hope I'll never have to be in a position to make such critical assessments. Your success — or failure — is not going to affect my life either way. I will follow your career with curiosity and interest, but your idea that we will be deeply close is probably another fantasy. I give it a year or two at best. There will be birthday and Christmas cards this year, Christmas cards the next, and then — silence. The war is over between us and I wish you well. Do you remember the night on the ship when I told you the story of Odysseus and Calypso? I was showing off,

147

my hair streaming in the wind. Odysseus rejected immortality with Calypso in order to return home. Was he not saying what you have said? "I have to be the centre of attention." I've often wondered, considering I was trying to hang onto you, why I chose to tell you that particular tale. I guess I was all along telling you to go back to Ithaca and chaste Penelope.

When we arrived at Piraeus, you had six letters from Hester waiting for you and I had letters from all my daughters. We were having our last breakfast on board, lingering a bit, partly because we knew we'd have to start paying again for food, and partly because we had been on the ship for nearly a month now and were about to plunge out into the unknown. Athens was only five miles away, under a brown haze of pollution. We were going to get our luggage off, clear it through Customs, leave it somewhere and zip up to the city to see if we had any mail at American Express. You were expecting a cheque and I had given that address to several friends. That night, we sailed for Crete.

I read my letters greedily, apologizing for reading them there at the table. The sight of the familiar handwriting made me cry. You got up and went to put your letters away. You said that you would read them at your leisure, after we were on the ferry.

Which you did. You had reserved us a first class cabin at the booking office, while I was at the bank changing money. I was surprised that we were going first class and you explained that we were "in transit" and should relax and enjoy ourselves. We got on the boat about five-thirty, but it wasn't due to sail until seven, so we explored the boat and stood on the deck a while, and then went down to our cabin, which was very nice.

I said I was going to have a shower before we sailed in case it was rough later on, and you nodded and stretched out on your bed. When I came naked out of the bathroom, you had Hester's letters spread out beside you and were deep into the first one.

You suggested that I might like to get dressed and go out to the lounge with the *Blue Guide*, have a drink; you'd prefer

148

to be alone for a little while. I had come out of the shower feeling very good and quite horny, thinking how organized you had been about all the luggage and phoning up Avis Rent-a-Car in Herakleion, and here we were in Greece and wouldn't it be nice to make love before dinner?

You suggested, before I had opened my praise-filled mouth, that I should get dressed and leave you alone. Your eyes were shining with tears. (Of course.) I put on a skirt and a blouse, picked up the *Guide* and my purse, and walked out.

For a while I went up on deck, just to look out at Piraeus and observe the scene on the boat. Most of the orange benches were already filled up with deck passengers — lots of young Europeans with backpacks and sleeping bags, sharing wine and cheese and olives, but some Greek families too. Everyone seemed to be *with* someone and I was all too aware that my "somebody" would rather be down in the cabin reading letters from his wife than up here in the Greek sunshine with me. Of course, you wanted to read your letters — you probably considered yourself very big to have put it off all day — but it hurt, Michael, it *hurt*. I had even been banished from the fucking cabin for which I, too, was paying twenty dollars. I kept telling myself to cheer up, but it wasn't much use. I wasn't really "seeing" anything (It took other crossings to make me realize how little I did see that night), so I went down to the lounge and ordered an expensive gin and tonic. I was sitting reading about Knossos, trying to get all those Minoan stages clear, when you suddenly appeared.

"There's a letter to you from Hester — it was enclosed in one of mine."

"Thanks," I said, reaching up casually without taking my eyes off my book, "I'll read it later."

"See you soon."

"Hmmmm."

You went back off down the hall. I ordered another two dollar gin and tonic. There were several very well-dressed Greek couples sitting around at little tables. I felt awkward and out of place, as I always do among such people. The women had on an awful lot of gold. The men had gold teeth and gold cufflinks.

I was about to go up on deck again — a steward had come through and announced the ship would sail in fifteen minutes — when you reappeared, freshly showered, your curly hair slicked down.

"Coming up to watch us leave?"

"I suppose so," I said, putting Hester's unopened letter in my book as a marker.

Up on deck, after I had taken a picture of you against the rail and you had taken one of me, you asked me what Hester had to say. I said I hadn't had time to read her letter yet, that as a matter of fact, I'd forgotten, I'd been so engrossed in the stuff on Knossos. I began to explain to you what an advanced civilization had been there.

"Hester's fine," you said, "she finds the heat pretty intense and she's lonely, but she's fine."

"That's nice," I said, and moved off to take a picture of a life preserver with the name of the boat printed on it in black letters: "KANDIA."

At dinner, which was as expensive as the drinks had indicated it would be, we sat at a round table laid for eight, but there was only another couple, who were Swiss, and ourselves. We drank a lot of Cretan wine and I, on drunken impulse, asked the woman, who was pretty and young and an artist, what she thought of a ménage à trois.

"I could never do zat," she said, and laughed. "It is not practical."

We bought another bottle of wine to take back to our cabin, but we never drank it. You asked me, furiously, why I had mentioned a ménage à trois to strangers.

"It was put as an abstract question. Europeans are more sophisticated about these things than we are. She was a pretty intelligent woman who had her own life. I wondered what she thought."

"You've been acting like a goddamn bitch ever since we got on board this ship."

"I don't like being told to leave my cabin."

"You don't like me getting letters from Hester."

"I don't mind that, but for you to stretch out on your bed and tell me to get out while you read them is too much!"

"I'd been waiting all day. I'd been arranging things and getting us tickets and all that."

"I could have done that; I'm not stupid. You wanted to do that. You have to be 'in control,' you say so yourself. You could have left some of that for me to do and gone off to a café somewhere and read your stupid letters."

"You wouldn't have liked that either."

"I would have liked that *better*."

"You're so disorganized you would have got us on the ferry to Rhodes or someplace."

"*Really?*"

We should have shut up. We said a lot of awful things, as usual, and I ended up scratching and hitting you, tossing Hester's (still unopened) letter to me out the porthole and being very sick in the bathroom.

In the morning, both of us had horrific headaches, but we were up on deck at six a.m. to see the "KANDIA" come into Crete.

I put my arm around you and told you I was sorry. You told me that I was a fucking bitch but was forgiven nevertheless. However, I would have to learn to control my jealousy of Hester or we could not possibly live in Greece together, even for three and a half months. You would get me settled and then move on to some other village and work quietly on your novel until it was time to leave.

Why didn't I say yes to that, Michael? Was it just because I wanted you to drive the car? We had had almost a month without letters from Hester. It had been a good month. Now the letters were going to begin and we would both feel pulled apart. I wasn't stupid; I knew what it was going to be like.

We found a man with a truck who would take my small trunk and the rest of our luggage up to the Avis Rent-a-Car. From the open back of the truck, we saw all the kids with backpacks, leaning forward, making their way up from the port to the town. "We're spoiled," I said.

"But we have books to get on with."

"True, too true." We were friends again, buddies, fellow-travellers, *artistes*. We weren't just in Crete to have *fun*, for God's sake, we were *serious*.

"Does she pee?" I once yelled at you when you were

extolling Hester's many virtues, "does she shit marsh-mallows?"

You said it was my "life experience" that made me so attractive to you. But it was precisely the result of that life experience that you hated so much: my children, my books (the fact of their publication). I know that it must be very hard to be thirty years old and have people ask you what you "do." (And people always will.)

"I'm a writer." This comes out a little too loud, a little too defiantly.

"Oh? Where have you published?" (Or what have you ——.)

"A few stories. I'm finishing up a novel right now."

And they smile their polite, contemptuous smiles.

And if they should then turn to the woman you are with and say, "And do *you* do anything?"

This is a materialist, empirical world. "Show me. Show me. Show me. Prove it." You are a man of enormous pride. How such a situation galls you. (And how it would probably gall most men.) No matter how often I said — and perhaps I was lying a little — that I considered us equals and the hell with what The World said — it was somehow my "fault" for putting you in such a humiliating position. ("*I* have to be the centre of the universe —" Well, you said it; you even wrote it down.) And the idea that The World might think you were with me in order to "get" someplace was equally awful. (And silly, in that instance because, what do I have? A handful of readers, a few hundred maybe, a very small reputation.)

You were at the movies alone one night. An artist whose show we had gone to — a painting of hers had been used as a cover for a re-issue of one of my novels — came in with some friends and sat down behind you. You heard her say, "Isn't that the fellow who lives with Rachel?" You used this as an example of the kind of thing you had to contend with. I agreed, but also said that the woman would probably not have remembered *my* name, if it hadn't been for the cover. If we'd just met once at a big opening night party.

You didn't like it, you said, it made you feel as though you had no identity of your own. I lost my temper.

"Stop feeling so sorry for yourself and *make* one!"

"What did you think of me," I said, "when you first saw me at your seminar?"

"I thought, 'Who's this chick to come in and pass judgment on our writing?'"

"And after you read my books?"

"I took it all back."

We were walking along Veikou the day before Christmas, laughing; you had an arm around each of us. Suddenly, Hester stuck her arm out as though it were draped over somebody's shoulder.

"Hester, what are you doing?"

"Practising."

"For what?"

"For when I find my other fellow. It doesn't have to stop at a ménage à trois."

I think I truly *liked* her, for the first time, at that moment. Maybe I even loved her.

"You're right!" I stuck my left arm out. People began to look at us as we walked along.

"A ménage à cinq."

"A sept." "A neuf!" "A onze!"

"You two think you're pretty fucking funny."

"We are, we are."

And yet, we all knew it was just a game, that you would make the rules and we would keep them. That was the kind of women we were, and you knew that too. In fact, you counted on it.

Down more, further yet: Hotel Agropolis, Hotel Astoria (Lux), Hotel Acteon, "Rent Rooms," Zimmer Frei, ENIK·ΔΩM; the last bend now, past (if we had known it) the vine-covered balcony outside your study; forward towards the sea, which was out of sight now; past the post office on the left, the bakery on the right; then, suddenly, right out onto the square, the fishboats dancing in front of us, the cliffs — "Aghia Sophia Buses Stop."

153

"Oh, Michael, this is where we must stay."

"Yes."

"I love you."

"I love you too. Aghia Sophia," you said, "all out. The end of the line."

One Sunday afternoon, we had a race. As we were crossing the river to get to the far beach, you suggested it. I was given a headstart because of your long legs. I ran and ran, ran as I hadn't run since I was a child, and you ran after me, laughing, letting me always remain just beyond your outstretched arms. And then, you caught me and ran with me, laughing, into the sea.

That was the day you took the picture of me in nothing but my hat, the picture I had enlarged and put in your birthday album. I took one of you pretending to be Poseidon, but I kept that one for myself. It is about three in the afternoon, in October, and our bodies are coated with light. In the photo, your hair looks almost blue.

You write in your letter tonight, "I owe you so much and didn't always treat you well. What to say: I'm sorry? I can't be sorry for the bad times because they can't be separated from the good. That old song comes back — remember me humming a few bars? 'If you leave me, I'll try to remember the good times — and just a little bit of rain / just a little bit of rain'."

I was in a bad mood from the moment I woke up on Boxing Day. I was homesick for the girls and I was worried because I hadn't got my period yet. And I had dreamt a curious dream about you and me and Hester and a party.

The party was given by Tall Girls — it may even have said that on the invitation. I went with you and, at the beginning, Hester was nowhere around. You stood in a doorway which led to the room where the party was taking place and flirted with a group of Tall Girls, all very pretty, who were taking tickets. I sat on a bench near the front door and waited for you to quit. Then someone engaged me in conversation and, when I looked up again, the doorway to the next room was empty and you had disappeared. I decided to go and look for you, and went into the other room. There was lots of music and dancing going on and I didn't see you at first. Then there you were, over at the far end of a sofa, with Hester squirming on top of you. What was horrible was that she was dressed exactly as I was, in a bright green sweater and jeans. Even the soles of her shoes were the same. I could see the look on your face and knew it because I had seen it so often when you were with me. I turned and ran away and then I woke up.

It was very early and the street outside, for once, was quiet. Hester had told me a dream she had down in Africa where you and she were making love and had identical star-shaped badges over your hearts. She said she has always felt some deep, almost mystical connection between the two of you. I said, "But it's *your* dream." Now this was mine. I didn't understand about the Tall Girls (I still don't), but the rest of it was very clear — a strong message from myself to myself.

You and she were going down to Africa very soon. The ménage would end; Hester would see to that. I got up and went to pee and could hear you both talking in low tones. Everybody was awake. I felt I couldn't go in, as you might be making love, and so I went back to my room, thoroughly depressed.

You came in around seven-thirty and lay down beside me, on top of the quilt.

"I do love you, you know. I wonder if you realize how much."

Hester came in and sat on the end of the bed. She said she'd heard me get up in the night and wondered if I'd finally got my period. I said, "No." And you frowned. You looked as though you were going to say something, exchanged a look with Hester, and then kept quiet.

"What's the matter with you two?"

"Nothing. We just worry about you, you know. It wouldn't be much fun having an abortion in a strange city."

"I wouldn't have one. Why would I have an abortion?"

Again, you two looked very uncomfortable and Hester

jumped up, offering to go make some breakfast.

"You couldn't be pregnant, could you?" you said.

"I could be, but I don't think so. I'm feeling very tired and grumpy, so that's a pretty sure sign I'm getting my period."

"I think I should tell you something, even though Hester asked me not to."

"*She's* pregnant."

"How could she be pregnant so soon?"

"It's not impossible."

"No. She's back on the pill. But she feels very strongly that if you got pregnant, she'd have to leave any arrangement the three of us had." You cleared your throat, "And I'd have to follow her."

"Why?"

"Because I'm the one who's said 'no children' all these years. Think how she would feel. She didn't want you to know because you're worried about your period and she says she's ashamed of the way she feels."

"I understand the way she feels, but it sounds an awful lot like blackmail to me. Why is she on the pill again, if she wants a child so badly?"

"Come on, Rachel, she couldn't be pregnant down in Africa, and then the big trek home and all that."

"I guess not. What you are really saying is not that Hester wants a child, but that she doesn't want *me* to have one."

"You've got three!"

"A child of yours."

"Yes."

I took in this information. You suggested that perhaps, next year, when Hester was well and truly pregnant, I might be allowed to have a child by you as well. I thanked you very much, fuming. Hester arrived with the eggs.

"L'oeuf," I said, "Love. Did you know that love in tennis originally meant egg: the egg, nought, nothing? The breakfast is very appropriate."

She looked at me, puzzled.
"I told her," you said, "I felt I had to."

You and Hester had been in the other room packing up a box of stuff you weren't going to take to Africa. I had been writing letters home. We'd had a little talk about the whole pregnancy thing. I told her what I had told you, that I didn't think for one minute I was pregnant. You suggested that perhaps, just for everybody's peace of mind, if I hadn't got my period by next week, I should go and have a test. Hester offered to come with me. She had been crying because of the way she felt.

"I don't know," I said, holding her hand. "I understand what you are feeling, but you're pretty determined. I think if you'd really wanted a child, you would've had one. But that's all past history; people change their minds. Just be sure the reason you feel so strongly about it now isn't because you think it will strengthen the bond between you and Michael. Babies aren't glue and they don't really hold relationships together if the relationship is ready to bust."

"Isn't that what you're doing?" you said, "Trying to get a firmer hold on me?"

"I've always wanted your child, you know that. But yes, right now you may be right."

We stared in on one another. It was all so bloody complex. We decided not to talk about it anymore that day and just get on with the things we had to do. We were hoping to get off to Mykonos the following day.

Around noon, Hester came in with you and said she was hungry and felt like spaghetti. I was still lying on my bed, writing. She loved spaghetti — we all did — and it was "your" dish, it would be easy for you to make.

"I'll make it tonight," you said.

"You can't, we're having communal turkey soup made Greek style — remember? With all that lot upstairs. 'Turkey avgolemono'."

"All right. I'll make spaghetti the night we come back from Mykonos."

"I feel like it now," she said.

157

"Lay off, Hester, I don't want to make it now. What if I go up and make some ham sandwiches and bring them down?" Your mother had sent us a food parcel.

Hester said, "I've got this terrible craving for spaghetti. I guess it's because I haven't had it in so long."

"Maybe *you* are pregnant," I said and we both laughed. There was a silence.

"I'll go make it," she said.

"That seems unfair, you made breakfast."

"It doesn't matter." (But I could see she was upset.)

"Oh, I'll come up and help you." I didn't want to, and I really should have stayed out of it, but two martyrs are better than one. "C'mon, Hester. I'll get dressed and we'll go have a spaghetti feast. There's one bottle of wine left somewhere. We'll have that too."

"I don't mind having spaghetti," you said, "as long as it's going."

I mocked you. "That's one of your favourite tricks, Michael — 'as long as it's going'." I was mad. I wanted to stay in bed and think about the consequences of being pregnant in Athens. I was feeling very sorry for myself.

Hester and I went upstairs. I was in a terrible temper.

"I don't think we should make him any," I said. "He's just trying to get away with as little work as possible — as usual."

"It doesn't matter. I would have made it anyway."

"Why don't you and I go out for spaghetti? I know there's a couple of Italian places in the Plaka."

She hesitated. "Oh — let's make it here, it's more homey."

There was a girl named Nancy sitting at the table, reading an old fashion magazine. She was from New Zealand and young and gay and pretty. The night before you had told her we had some dope, which I felt was really unwise of you (plus the fact that there was hardly any left).

"Where's Michael?" she said. "He promised me a joint and it never materialized."

"He'll be up later on."

"Which one of you is his girlfriend?" she said. "I can't quite make it out."

"Hester's his wife," I said. "I suppose I'm his girlfriend, although sometimes it seems the other way around."

Hester blushed, but I didn't care. Nancy began telling us her troubles with her boyfriend. He had given her a ticket home from London to Australia because he didn't want to live with her anymore. Oh well, she'd get over it.

You came up. It was obvious you were a little stoned.

"Where's that joint you promised me?" Nancy said.

"What time's lunch?" you said.

"Oh, in about twenty minutes," Hester said.

"Well, these ladies don't usually indulge in the middle of the day, so if you'd like to come downstairs, we've just got time for a quick one."

"He won't help," I said to Hester, "and he treats us as though we were his *mothers* — 'What time's lunch?' — or worse, *servants* — and then he takes her downstairs to smoke what little dope there is left. *He* doesn't care — *he's* not taking any chances carrying dope down to Dar. *God*!!"

"Are you sure you aren't just jealous of Nancy? She's very pretty."

"Hester, she's a child. I'm not jealous of *children*. I'm mad that he's so openly exploiting us and enjoying it."

"Oh, you know what he's like when he's stoned."

"Yes. Stupid. He's not *that* stoned yet. He knows what he's doing. Now he's got an audience of three. 'Look how clever I am, I've got two attractive women upstairs cooking for me and here we are downstairs chatting and smoking up.' He's not interested in Nancy sexually. He just wants to impress her. How free he is, what a man of the world he is, how much he is still *of her generation*."

"That's pretty hard on him."

"I don't think so. I think he's a shit when he behaves like that. Cock of the walk."

But then we began laughing. We set two places, one for each of us, and uncorked the wine and poured ourselves each a glass. We were just sitting down when you and Nancy came up, stoned.

"Hey, hey, smells good. Where shall I sit?"

"Wherever you like," I said. "Nancy, do you want some spaghetti?"

"No thanks, I'm trying to slim." She got a dish of yoghurt out of the fridge.

"Good spaghetti," I said to Hester. "Pass me some more

cheese, please, if you can reach it."

You were still smiling your silly stoned smile, disbelieving.

"Nancy," I said, "would you like a glass of wine? Michael doesn't usually indulge in the middle of the day, but perhaps you'd like some?"

Uncomfortably, she said yes, she would like some. (Later, she told me that you said to her downstairs, "Well, at least *you're* on my side, aren't you, Nancy?" and she had told you, it had nothing to do with her.)

"Where's my spaghetti?"

"Help yourself," Hester said.

"Where's my goddamn plate?" (But you were still laughing. You still thought it was a terrific joke.)

"You know where the plates are, serve yourself."

"Serve myself! Jesus!"

But it was all a game to you, you loved it.

I went downstairs directly after lunch and was putting on my new boots, thinking I should get out of there and take a walk, when you appeared. You came and put your arms around me.

"You fucking bitch, you're a terrible woman."

But you were smiling, I could see how much you were enjoying it.

"Don't touch me. Let me alone."

You shrugged and went back out the door.

Later, as I walked on Philoppapou Hill, I heard you and Hester call to me, but I didn't care. I hated you. I hated being put in the position of mother/servant to you while you showed off. I hated Hester for going out walking with you. I hated the idea of an abortion. I hated everything. I had worked up a really good hate by the time I came back from my walk.

Then I got out a bottle of ouzo and smoked some of your dope and lay on my bed, thinking.

Labyrinth: a maze, a place full of lanes and alleys.

There was a full moon the night you left for Africa. I took you out for dinner at a Japanese restaurant near where I lived and the waitress, who was also a part-owner, turned out to be from Vancouver. She asked if we were married. People were always asking us if we were married. Of course the Greeks will ask you anything; their curiosity is boundless, but other people asked us too. Perhaps the tensions, the vibrations were ambiguous between us. I was tempted to shout, "MARRIED?? I'M HIS MOTHER!" but I knew you wouldn't find that funny. We took a cab over to the city centre, you with your head out the window, getting your last fill of the dark shape of the Acropolis under the moon, as we sped along Dionysius Areopagite. You deposited me outside Zonar's and went to get your pack from the cheap hotel where you had moved after Hester had left. I ordered Nescafé and tried not to think about what it was going to be like when you were well and truly gone. Tomorrow night you would be in Addis Ababa; the following night in Dar, safe in Hester's arms. It was cold out and we both had on our caps and mittens. I had never thought of Greece as *cold*. The wind was coming down from Russia, my landlady said. I should have paid more attention in geography class. I was glad I wasn't on Crete, with no heat and the hallway open to the roof.

I saw you come in before you located me. There you were in your knitted cap and big beard, bowed under by an enormous pack, and I thought first, what an idiot you looked among the marble tables and white-coated waiters, and then, how much I loved you for that unpretentiousness, that ability or refusal to be other than you were. To not be *embarrassed* in such a place, or at least awkward, as I so often was.

You were very very excited. You were off on another adventure. Africa! Now that was really the "Other." You saw me, grinned, and carefully made your way over.

"Did you order me coffee?"

"Not yet."

You sat down facing the door, as you always did. You always wanted to sit that way because you said you liked watching people come and go. I think you didn't like having your back to the door.

161

"You shouldn't have chosen this table."

"Why not?"

You pointed behind me. There was a large mirror in which your handsome face was perfectly reflected.

"Narcissus drowned," I said. "Try and get the waiter."

"I still see you driving away in the cab the night I left, waving. I think of you often and miss you. My Barcelona poster hangs on the wall in the living room. Remember getting it? Them? I do."

Remember this? Remember that? Oh take it, Jesus, take it. Jesus, take it.

Hester went back, then you left, and then I was alone. There was a certain relief. The day after the Big Scene, I lay on my bed wondering why I had done it, why I had been so mean to Hester when it was really you I was so angry at. I wrote you both a long letter and left it at American Express, and the next day, you left me a reply, you writing on one side of the page; Hester on the other. "Let's all meet for supper on Thursday night." You mentioned that you had decided to move up your leaving date. I went over to the Hotel Cleo. Only Hester was there. You were out at a travel agent's. I apologized to her and began to cry. That's when she said that she knew the whole ménage had been a fantasy all along. She mentioned a friend of hers who had tried it and had ended up with a broken heart.

When you came in, very high because you were about to get moving again, you were surprised to see me, but suggested we all go out for dinner. We met in the late afternoon and went out for dinner every day until you left. We were all very quiet, very subdued and very polite to one another. We had our pictures taken, you in the middle, by one of the old photographers on the Acropolis. One night, I told Hester that I was afraid to be alone again. She said, "I'll be alone again too, sometime." I wondered if she really believed that and what your life together was going to be like from now on.

162

We talked a bit about the plan to join up down in Africa once my book was done. To "visit" became the word. I tried to imagine what it would be like never to make love to you again. I understood why Hester had asked you to sleep with her, "one last time," all those long months ago. She wanted you to feel how much she still loved you. It wasn't sexual — it was beyond that. I felt very close to her those last few days. We probably could have been, in the end, good friends. I envied her generosity. There was nothing smug about it. She was like someone who has just come out of a long illness, a bad one, but not fatal, and is so delighted to be alive that she loves the whole world. I gave her a pair of turquoise and silver earrings the day she left.

(But I also gave you the special freighter and Greece photo album and I included, enlarged even, the photo of me sitting nude on the beach. I wasn't just reminding you, I was reminding *her*. I wonder when you will take that one out and throw it away.)

Latakia was our final stop before Piraeus. The itinerary called for Beirut, but this was changed, perhaps because of the troubles. I had figured out from the daily reports of wind, weather and mileage that by this time we had covered over five thousand nautical miles since leaving New York. We really had been on a voyage. A plane could have done it in hours, but it had taken us nearly a month. I liked that; I liked that slow, almost dream-like sense of moving along over maps. Air travel always seemed to me a perversion of the real reasons for travelling, which are, I think, connected with the reasons why we dream. To be flung into the air like a tennis ball and come down in another court is awful. Our bodies and minds are shocked. A bruising of our sensibilities has taken place. I hate it.

There were over a hundred ships in the harbour, either waiting for a berth or waiting to be off-loaded onto barges. Ships from everywhere. Russian ships, Polish ships, ships from Greece and Scandinavia and the U.S., from Cyprus. Ships flying Panamanian or Liberian flags, so Christ knows where they were from. Ships from Red China. Waiting for the agent to come on board, we stood next to the steward, who had binoculars and a flag book. It was an amazing sight. We could see the city beyond. The steward said it was famous for its tobacco. Every so often jet fighter planes went screaming overhead. When the agent came on board, he tried to discourage us from going ashore. Please, why didn't we wait? The ship was supposed to move in the next morning. Sheeplike, all the others elected to stay on board. You asked if he could arrange to have a boat sent out for us around two or three. He said, "Yes." But Björn said, "Don't count on it — that guy doesn't want to be bothered." We got all ready nevertheless. It was so frustrating to be only a mile away from Syria and not to be able to get to it. We packed our bathing suits, some apples and oranges, some money, hats to wear against the sun, which was fierce, a borrowed thermos full of water that was safe to drink — but no maps, because we hadn't expected to stop there. We went and sat in the lounge where the King of Norway stared benignly down on us. No boat. The other passengers were very patronizing about the whole thing. They kept echoing Björn, saying, "Don't count on it, don't count on it," until finally I said to the Widow (the first time I had really lost my temper with any of them), "You know, I get the distinct feeling you don't *want* us to get off." She said, "What an extraordinary idea!" and got very huffy.

Two-thirty p.m. No boat. Three p.m. Everyone had gone for naps. It was very hot. You went up on deck to shout and wave at any small boat that came near. This was when Shay Weinstein stuck her head out the porthole and yelled up, "Michael, Michael, I'm *trying* to get some sleep." You yelled back, "*I'm* trying to get to Latakia!" And you succeeded, by God. You yelled to me, "Let's go." You got one of the crew to lower the gangplank over the prow of this *tiny*, tiny fish boat and we jumped aboard, me terrified, but you were there to hold me, and cautiously, we made our way around to the stern and putt-putted away in triumph. The Widow's astonished face appeared for a moment at a porthole and we stuck out our tongues and waved.

164

Our triumph? The small boat picked its way among the freighters, Lilliputians among Brobdignags, and reached the port. The fisherman brought out a big torn straw hat — the kind one might have put on a donkey or a horse in the old days — and taking your sailor hat off your head, gave you the straw hat.

"No, no," you said, smiling. "No thanks."

The boatman just laughed and said something liquid and incomprehensible, counted his money and indicated we should get out. Some rough-looking fellows hauled me up onto the concrete pier. There was noise and confusion and men everywhere, and what signs there were, were in Arabic. What had we done? The soldiers at the port gate spoke a little English, so we explained that we wanted a hotel. "Hotel? Want Hotel?" They leaned on their guns and smiled. "Let's splurge and get something really nice," you said to me. They commandeered a van which was leaving the port, pointed to us, said something, and we were invited to get in.

"Hotel. Want cheap hotel?"

"Nice," we said, "nice hotel."

"Nice." He nodded and away we went. It wasn't going to be so bad after all.

After a while, we were set down in the midst of a hubbub of noise and narrow streets full of small shops and Arabic signs.

"I think we are not exactly in the 'nice' area," I said. "This is a bazaar." It all looked pretty strange and pretty dirty, and we started to walk on. A man in a purple silk shirt detached himself from the crowd.

"You want hotel?"

We hesitated.

"I work Ramses Hotel across street."

We looked at each other and decided to follow him, with justified misgivings. The room had clean sheets, but was very hot, and the bathroom was filthy. Yet we decided to stay — out of cowardice, I think. What the hell, we had our own towels and washcloths and our thermos. I asked him to wash out the bathroom.

"Right away."

The owner appeared at the door. He said his name was Abdhul, which seemed only fitting, and he invited us to his office for beer. I explained about the bathroom. He said it was no trouble and would be cleaned up right away. He said he was an "engineer" and had not slept at all the night before because he was too busy "drawing." You asked if he had a map and he said certainly, of course, only too happy to oblige, and rooted through his drawers until he found one.

A portrait of a fat, prosperous-looking Syrian hung over his desk. There was a black band across it.

"Fadder dead," he said. "Come. I show you my fine Oriental saloon." We followed him across the dingy unswept hall to a door, which he unlocked with great ceremony. There were a lot of stiff, heavily-brocaded chairs in blue and silver, a reproduction of the Mona Lisa of all people on one wall, and a huge portrait of Fadder on the other. We were very appreciative (Was this the Middle East equivalent of our old fashioned parlour?) and he was enormously pleased. He offered to take us out to the "plage" in his fine van for a swim. He was too helpful; both paranoid by nature, he made us suspicious. Was this a real hotel? What would an "engineer" be doing running a decrepit joint like this? *Ramses* Hotel? *Abdhul*? Wasn't it all just a little too pat? Perhaps it was a brothel that specialized in foreigners. Perhaps the soldiers at the port were in on it, and the man in the green van which had so "conveniently" appeared just at the right moment. Perhaps we were going to be made to perform unnatural, unspeakable acts in front of prosperous traders. Or *with* them. "This is the Middle East," I said. "*You* won't be immune." I had my period. Was that taboo? Would they kill me when they found out they had touched me and I had my period? Would they kill us both?

"Listen, Michael," I said, "let's get out of here." We were upstairs in our room, frightening each other and laughing at the same time. "That guy Abdhul gives me the creeps. Maybe he's going to sit naked on one of those fancy chairs and I'll have to suck him off."

"Or I will."

"Or both of us."

"I have never felt so far from home."

"Me either."

The bathroom had not been touched. It stank of pee.

"There must be other places to stay. This is a big town —

a city really."
"Yeah. How do we find them?"
"Maybe they're marked on the map. If not, we'll find the main street and walk along it."
You got out Abdhul's map.
"Oh no!"
"What's the matter?"
"Look."
The map was in Arabic and German.

Months later, all we had to do was say, "Latakia," and we'd both start to laugh hysterically. It became as much a part of our personal jargon as "Take it, Jesus, take it." It became a private metaphor for any situation in which, for whatever reasons, you were in over your head. In the end, it became a metaphor for you and me. We survived the real Latakia and, in fact, we had a pretty good time there, all things considered, but I think the gods were with us — or at least watching out. Your unerring sense of direction helped and the general absurdity of the whole situation. We didn't move from the Ramses Hotel and we even, in twenty-four hours, got to like the bustle of the bazaars, the glimpses of old men playing backgammon in the coffee houses, the women in black veils, the young girls in military uniforms giggling at your dark good looks, your height.

We found the promenade and walked the length of it, wondered how on earth we were going to locate the ship, which would have moved, and what we would do if we couldn't find it. We ate in a huge open-air restaurant, which also seemed to be a casino, by the sea. We smoked a hubble-bubble which was brought to our table and lit, and the long snakey pipe handed ceremoniously to us. People all around, women and men, were smoking. We both began to feel a little dizzy and wondered if we could possibly, openly, be smoking hash. The man at the next table spoke French and you asked him. He laughed. "No. But when you first smoke this way, you 'turn a little'."

I held your hand tightly as we found our way through the dark streets, back to our hotel. Then you went out again to explore and I went to bed, exhausted. Perhaps five minutes passed before there was a knock on the door.

"Michael?" (I was almost asleep.)

"Could you give beer glasses please? I must to wash them." It was the voice of the man in the purple silk shirt.

I did not reply. Eventually, I heard his steps go slowly back down the stairs. I was not even frightened; the whole thing was too absurd.

"Listen," I said, "we've got to find the boat." We had been to the Norwegian Consulate — a French-speaking student showed us the way — but no one was there, except some blonde children riding tricycles on the verandah and two Syrian maids. Now we stood on a crowded street outside the French Tourist Office, which was closed. It looked as though it had been closed for a long, long time. Latakia was not really what you would call a tourist town. We still had only an Arabic/German map. What if the boat sailed without us?

"Michael, we've got to find that boat."

"Shut up a minute, Rachel. We'll find it."

"How? How?"

"Somebody here speaks English. There's always somebody."

"Good luck."

Tapping your foot, you scanned the passing scene. The night before, in the bazaar, we had bought you a blue hat to replace the white one which was taken by the fisherman who brought us into port. You looked a bit foolish because the brim came down too low, but the sun was climbing towards noon. Suddenly, you stepped forward and put your hand on the arm of a prosperous-looking Syrian in a Western-style suit.

"Excuse me," you said, "do you speak English?"

The man beamed, "Why, but certainly I do."

We had been entertained with sweetmeats and coffee and now our friend the Syrian, the Singer Sewing Machine representative for Latakia, was on the phone locating the ship for us. He would write a note in Arabic for the soldiers at the port. No problem. Rest assured.

"Somebody is looking after us."

"God bless Mr. Singer and his wonderful machine."

Three Chinese sailors in straw hats, with bands on their sleeves (Chairman Mao had died two days before), halted in a doorway directly across from the Singer shop.

"Look," you said. They had spread a map against the wall and were chattering away, shaking their heads.

"Do you suppose it's the same map we have?"

I still see the sad worried faces of those three Chinese and it always makes me laugh. If it was difficult for us, what on earth was it like for them?

We agreed that it was the language barrier that confounded us, more than the heat or the crowds, or the sense that we were in an area that was politically volatile. Always before, we had been able to at least *sound out* a word. This stuff looked like decoration. Very pretty on shops and street signs, but there was no way to decipher it. For two such highly verbal people as you and me, it was a kind of "epiphany." How much we depended on language, on verbal interchange, for our security. We were uneasy and disoriented in this place, where what we heard and what we saw printed was utterly incomprehensible. A baby must feel like that when it first realizes sounds are being made which the giants around him understand, but which he does not understand. I keep trying to remember what it was like. And to pick up a book and not be able to read! One should be able to remember that, wouldn't you think? I came close in Latakia. And there, as the student wrote out the name of a restaurant for us, I realized with a shock that they even wrote in a different direction! How had that happened? Where, when, had the shift taken place? I stared in wonder at his pen moving across the paper.

Since then, I have found out a little more why some

people write in one direction and others in another (the earliest Greek scribes determined the direction of their writing by the way it best fit into the space. Often, too, the writing went in both directions) —

Hello, Michael.

UOY ƎЯA WOH

But at the same time I whispered, "Now I know we're through the looking glass."

And later, when we had been back to the ship and returned to Latakia in a tender with the others, for the boat had to stay an extra day, we took a taxi out to Ras Shamra, where they discovered the most ancient alphabet in the world. We stood on that dusty hillside looking at royal palaces and archives, a temple dedicated to the god Baal, and tried to imagine the layers and layers of history buried there, one on top of the other. A name from the Bible: the Canaanites. We each bought a copy of the alphabet of Ugarit, which showed the correspondence with Latin and Arabic. The guide spoke French, but very little English, so his talk was difficult to follow: "The died mans slept here." Some king was buried in "the fatal position." Most of the great treasures from the dig were at Damascus or Aleppo, or in the Louvre — the carved ivory, the rich objects of gold, the statuettes and arms of bronze, vases of alabaster and baked pottery tablets upon which were set down inventories, myths and poems. The guide told us, apologetically, that we would have to use our imagination. I had a piece of clay in my hand, a small replica into which had been pressed the thirty cuneiform letters of the Ugaritic alphabet:

A △ △ __

B ◺ __ ◺ __

The first letter of the "most ancient alphabet" seemed to me *always* to be greed, aquisitiveness, the desire to plunder and possess. The heat had made me dizzy. Hundreds of white moths danced over the landscape and I could hear the voices of schoolchildren down below. I sat on a bit of ruined wall

170

and let the others go ahead. You came back to find me.

"What's the matter, Rachel?"

"Oh, the whole question of language, of communication, it's impossible. Why didn't we just stick to gestures and grunts."

"I'm surprised at you, of all people."

"Trying to make things clear. We invent alphabets and language systems in order to make things *clear*. But it doesn't really help. Once you get beyond letters, into words, into emotions and ideas, it doesn't help at all."

"That's nonsense."

"Is it? Nothing ever changes. People don't get any *better* as their language gets more sophisticated. And people who speak the same language don't even speak the same language. You. Me. All of us. All just make the same *sounds*. That's even more terrifying than the first three hours in Latakia. At least here you *know* the language is different."

"People have to *try* and get through to one another."

"Why?"

"Because they do. Because it's in their nature to want to."

("Goodbye, Rachel. I love you. It was a Latakia.")

We thanked the Singer Sewing Machine man. "Welcome," he said. "Is nothing. I am Syrious. We are all alike."

Well, Michael, now you are part of my "archaeology" and I am a part of yours (unless you destroy all traces of me for Hester's sake). Sun down. Moon up. Time for me to brush my hair, put on a dress and go down into the square. For the next few months, I intend to live quietly and very simply. The girls will be here, and Robert too, in July. I will go up to Athens to meet them and the girls and I will hug and Robert and I will lean forward and kiss each other awkwardly, the way we always do, not sure quite where to put our bodies. He'll love this place. He's always going on about the "aesthetics of the flesh." Meanwhile, I will enjoy this rare spaciousness and keep on observing. I don't know what to do about my life except to keep on going and to try to make "progress." It seems to take a whole lifetime to learn how to live, and then we need another one to put it all into practice.

Down now from the rooftop, ten steps. Then thirteen to the street. From up here the sea, right now, looks as smooth and grey as a skating rink. Life calls. Goodbye, Michael. I love you, my dear. I'm going skating.

And remember, the best revenge is writing well.

TALONBOOKS — FICTION IN PRINT 1979